C.V. HUNT'S

HORRORAMA

THREE NOVELETTES BY

A.S. Coomer
Lucas Mangum
Matt Harvey

Table of Contents

INTRODUCTION

When I decided to take ownership of Grindhouse Press I had a few ideas of what type of books I wanted to publish. The original term 'grindhouse' was used to reference a wide array of films from the 60s and 70s. They were horror. They were gritty. They were action packed. Sometimes the storylines were bonkers (ex. *Driller Killer*). They were sometimes referred to as B movies: shot with a low budget and cranked out as quickly as possible. This was the basic concept of Grindhouse Press in the beginning and I wanted to expand on it.

As much as I love grindhouse films I also enjoy the video nasties from the 80s and low budget, shot-on-video films. Films that didn't answer to anyone. Too extreme or transgressive? So what. That is what made those films lovable in my eyes. No major production companies telling the director what they could or couldn't film. No one telling them to rewrite the script or tons of footage lost on the cutting room floor. They were raw and you were either into them or you weren't.

One of the first horror films I can recall watching was *Basket Case* at the ripe age of eight or nine years old. *Basket Case* is the story of a demented and deformed conjoined twin who's separated from his brother and decides to go on a killing spree as revenge. I feel like if you're reading this then I don't need go into great detail about the movie since you've probably already seen it. But to this day I think Frank Henenlotter is one of the best horror directors. His films are campy and fun. The story lines are ridiculous but there's always an undertone of social commentary. Come on . . . *Frankenhooker?*

I grew up in the middle of a cornfield . . . literally. And the nearest city was barely a city. My dad rented VHS tapes like they were going out of style which, as you know, they did. I wasn't fortunate enough to have a local horror movie host in my area. I was thrilled to discover, after moving to Dayton, they used to have their very own horror movie host, Dr. Creep, who has unfortunately passed on. I grew up watching Elvira. Don't get me wrong. I wouldn't trade Elvira for the world. But there is a great level of charm that comes with having your own local horror movie weirdo, spouting ridiculous one-liners and guiding you through some crazy black-and-white film they rescued from public domain.

For a few years our local drive-in would show triple features of classic grindhouse films every Friday and Saturday night through the month of October: *The Texas Chainsaw Massacre*, *Evil Dead*, and *Last*

House on the Left to name a few. I'd rush home on Friday to eat dinner, layer up on clothes, pop some popcorn (because I'm a cheap bastard), and show up at the drive-in early because they had employees running around dressed as Freddy Krueger or Leatherface, tormenting the movie goers. And then last year they didn't do it.

My intention this year was to hit up the local Horrorama. Twenty-four hours of non-stop horror movies at a smaller indoor theater. But then . . . 2020 happened. In case you've been living under a rock these past few months, there's a global pandemic happening. I don't imagine the Horrorama will be happening this year. And if it does, I won't be attending it.

The concept behind this anthology is a tribute to those horror movie marathons. Three stories, not exactly related in any way, other than my love for those grindhouse, video nasties, and shot-on-video horror movies. Three novelettes that could be read in the time it would take to watch three movies. I guess that's subjective to how quick or slow one reads. So pop some popcorn, kick back, and enjoy the ride.

C.V. Hunt

August 2020

Store-All Self-Storage

A.S. Coomer

To all the weirdos
With love.

WHAT A WEIRD WORLD THE world of storage unit rentals turned out to be. On a whim, in the doldrums between writing projects, I called the number I found in the classifieds. Part-time help needed for front desk work and "light security."

"Yellow," the voice answered.

"Blue," I said.

There was a pause.

"Stor-All Self-Storage," the voice said.

"Yes. I hear you're looking for some part-time help."

"Hold on," the voice said. "Jimmy. Jimmy, phone."

There was a scuffling of the phone being transferred to Jimmy.

"This is Jimmy."

"Yes, Jimmy. I'm calling in regards to your ad in the *Blade*."

"Eight an hour. Nights and weekends. Applications in person."

The phone clicked dead.

Well, I thought.

•••

Stor-All Self-Storage was at the end of South, where the few shitty houses still standing all lean and are nearly all boarded up. Its closest neighbors were grain docks for the river barges and bare, empty fields littered with trash.

Toledo.

I pulled into the small parking lot in front of the little trailer front office. The place was completely enclosed with a high barbed wire-topped chain link fence. Rust glittered like bloody diamonds in the faint drizzle.

I remember wondering if I really wanted to spend hours of my life, time I could've spent reading or writing or jacking off, at this dump.

I can read here, I reasoned. If it's only nights and weekends, I'm sure this place will require as much work as a . . . bras on ten-year olds? Sprinklers in the rain?

I racked my brain for something funny that didn't require a lick of work. Nothing of note came. The blockage continued.

The doorknob was cold and wet and stuck. I tried it several times before giving up and banging on the flimsy door.

Standing on the shaky wooden steps, I felt the trailer move with the man's steps.

The door opened and a pale, balding incantation of Jabba the Hutt squinted out into the mist at me.

"Yeah?" the man asked.

The voice was unmistakable despite the unlit stogie clenched between his teeth: Mr. Yellow from the phone.

"Afternoon. I'm here to apply for the part-time job." I extended my hand but Mr. Yellow didn't take it.

"Jimmy," he called, not taking his beady eyes off me.

The trailer shook again and Jimmy, a near mirror image of Mr. Yellow, stood looking over Mr. Yellow's shoulder at me.

"Yeah?" Jimmy asked.

"I'm here to apply for the job."

"Eight an hour. Nights and weekends—" he started.

"I know. You told me on the phone."

Both men seemed to suck in their breaths at my interruption. They were too identical not to be brothers. Two fat, pale, sickly-yellow Jabbas.

I've got to get this job, I thought.

•••

I signed and dated the stained and crinkled application and tried to slide it across the particleboard desk to Jimmy Clobs. There was too much other shit on his desk—crushed soda cans, fast food wrappers, receipts, various documents, a paperweight statue of a standing bear with a bald eagle resting on its shoulder—for this to happen. I handed it across the desk instead.

Jimmy Clobs, with his his brother Clarence Clobs (whom I still can only think of as Mr. Yellow) reading over his shoulder, scanned my application. His eyes were almost closed they were slitted so tight. They were a long time with the single page stock application.

I was overqualified. I knew that. I don't think a GED or, God willing, a high school diploma, something of a holy grail in Toledo, were required for the work the job demanded.

With a clicking noise somewhere deep within the fat folds of his face, Jimmy Clobs let the paper float onto the desk.

"You'll start tomorrow night. Nine to seven. No drinking. No drugs. No fucking up," Jimmy Clobs said.

I smiled. God help me, I actually smiled.

•••

No *training required*, the ad should've read.

No *supervision required*, the ad should've also read.

No *work required*, I thought the classified ad should've read.

I was wrong.

Jimmy Clobs was already gone for the weekend when I got there that next night, Friday. Mr. Yellow had his legs up on the cluttered desk in a cloud of cheap cigar smoke.

"'Bout time," he huffed at me when I entered the little trailer, knocking first, of course.

I checked the watch on my wrist.

8:45pm.

I decided not to make an issue of it. Not the greatest first day on the job impression.

I took off my raincoat and folded it over my arm.

"If anything happens, call the police," Mr. Yellow said.

When he stood, he actually had to use both of his hands to hoist his massive legs off the desk, and half of the shit on the desk went with his legs. He didn't notice or, more likely, didn't deign the mess important enough to pick up.

"Got a number for Jimmy, uh, Mr. Clobs, I mean, for me to call in case of an emergency?"

"Call the police," Mr. Yellow said.

He brushed by me but stopped at the door. There was a faded *Hustler* centerfold scotch taped to the back of the door, which I hadn't noticed the day before. Mr. Yellow stuck his grubby sausage fingers into his pants and fished out a set of keys. He tossed them to me and I caught them.

Mr. Yellow smiled as if he hadn't expected me to be quick enough for such an action.

"See you in the morning," he said and shut the door behind him.

I stared at the keys in my hands. There were three of them. Three. I figured there should've been hundreds of keys, one for each of the little roll-up mesh steel-doored units.

I wasn't told I had to make rounds. I wasn't told I couldn't sleep. I wasn't told what to do if a customer knocked on the door or lost his key. Nothing.

I plopped down onto the torn leather seat behind the desk and stared at the blonde licking the redhead's clitoris on the back of the trailer's door.

This is gonna be great, I thought.

•••

I was four stories deep into *The Short Works of Leo Tolstoy* when the limo pulled up to the electronic gate. I watched from a little hole I made in the foggy front window. The driver's side window smoothly rolled down and a jacketed arm emerged to enter several digits into the keypad. The gate jerked into motion and slid open. The window rolled up and the car disappeared into the murk of the storage unit maze.

I ripped a corner off the first piece of paper I grabbed from the desk. To my amusement, it was my application. I marked my page with the corner and tossed my book on the chair. I stepped out into the night just as the gate finished locking itself back into the closed position.

I lit a cigarette and strolled through the shroud of mist to the gate.

I peered through the holes in the fence, but the limo was gone, around one of the corners, out of sight.

I inhaled on the cigarette and coughed.

Tastes like shit, I thought. Smells like shit too.

I started smoking because I thought it was something writers were supposed to do. I pictured Elmore Leonard's bug-eyed testicle head peering up from his typewriter in a cloud of menthol.

It gave my hands something to do because Lord knows they weren't typing anything of worth. The blockage still reigned supreme.

I stubbed out the cigarette with my boot and jangled the set of keys Mr. Yellow had given me between my hands. There was a key slot in the gate. I hesitated before trying the first of the keys, trying to convince myself it was probably one of my job duties, though unstated, to do a round or two through the place every night.

As luck would have it, shit luck I now know it to have been, the first key turned easily in the lock and I slid open the gate enough to pass through. I eased it shut again and lit another cigarette, determined to find or, at least, fabricate an enjoyment for the things.

There were weak orange security lights every fifty yards or so. They hung higher than I thought necessary and the light that found its way to the cracked and pockmarked pavement was of little use. I stood listening for clues as to which direction the limo had headed under the first of the security lights. I squinted my eyes and craned my left ear, the far better functioning of my Dumbo appendages, toward the starless night sky. The light looked like a hazy pumpkin head of some leering autumnal deity.

I thought I heard a whimper in the night. A slight noise it was. As soon as I thought I heard it, it dissipated and I wasn't sure I had actually heard anything.

I took the first left and started down the long, narrow lane of shut up little garages. I couldn't see the limo but the sound had come from that general direction. I finished the cigarette and mentally patted myself on the back for not gagging or coughing.

I walked as quietly as I could. I chided myself about this. I was the security guard, after all. I reached the end of the lane and turned right, following the rusted fence. The place was much larger than I had expected. The security lights looked like blinking buoys in some murky Lake Erie nightscape. The horn of a barge from the nearby Maumee River sounding as I walked only increased this vision.

I was not protected from the wind on this side of the units. I blinked back tears and wiped my runny nose. The farther I walked, the fewer security lights shone until not one shone and a heavy blanket of wet night hung over everything. It reminded me of the time I'd built a fort out of quilts and lawn chairs in the backyard and, too preoccupied with my Batman comics, was caught out in a torrential downpour.

I walked on in darkness, the gray sides of the concrete block storage unit buildings seeming like sleeping beasts on the night's shore. My cigarette had long since burned out but I hadn't noticed. I walked with the stub of it hanging from my bottom lip, lost in my thoughts.

Why hadn't I become the big, famous writer I'd always supposed I'd become? Weren't my vampire stories subtle enough? Didn't they have more restraint than any of the other gore splashers? Didn't Dr. Hall find the second draft of my Victorian comedy novel, *Shrugging Buggies*, "hilarious and well crafted?" I mean, he wrote that on the manuscript. The red ink flashed in my mind and I retraced the shapes of the letters smiling in reverie. I'd been so proud.

I came to an abrupt stop in the harsh glow of the limo's taillights. My breath caught in my throat and the cigarette dropped from my lip.

•••

The driver's side rear door of the limo stood open, as did the door to a unit some five feet from it. There was a faint green glow emanating from within the unit.

I opened my mouth but found it too dry to speak. I cleared my throat and tasted the nasty cigarettes.

"Hello," I called.

There was no response.

I stood still, quiet, listening. A faint wet noise came from in there. Like the sound of milking a cow or a baby suckling from the teat.

I called again but my voice wouldn't rise above a whisper.

"Mmm."

There was a whimper from in there. The suckling sound did not abate.

I felt dumb, numb, my feet heavy or glued to the insides of my boots, my boots concreted to the pavement. I longed for the lesbian scene and the dingy interior of the front office trailer.

Idiot, I thought. *All you had to do was sit there and read and hopefully learn something from old Leo. Now, God only knows what you've stumbled on.*

With a will I didn't know I had, I stepped forward.

•••

What I saw left me slack jawed and confused. Surrounded by a pulsing green glow, a woman in a tight black dress was being enveloped. That's the only word for it: enveloped. Just the faintest wisp of her blonde hair was visible. The top part of her head wasn't there. I'm not saying her brain was out or anything like that. Just the top part of her head wasn't there. Like it had never been there.

The woman whimpered again. Her mouth was slack as if she was asleep.

The green pulsated and more of her head disappeared.

I felt sick. I wanted to throw up the shitty McDonald's hamburger I had eaten in my car on the way to Stor-All. I didn't throw up though. Not then anyway.

I stepped from the door to the storage unit and leaned back against the cool concrete blocks.

Call the police. That's what Mr. Yellow told me. If anything happens, call the police.

I imagined how the tape of that distress call would sound.

"911, what's your emergency?"

"There's a glowing green cloud making a woman disappear. Please send help."

"Sir, 911 isn't a phone line. Crank callers will be prosecuted."

There was another flash from the open door of the storage unit. I saw it reflected off the black tinted windows of the limo.

Christ, I thought.

That's when the driver's side door of the limo opened and a man in a dark suit stepped out. I was too stunned to move. The man's shoes were polished so well I could almost make out the reflection of the blonde and the blob on them.

"It's best you leave, sir," the man said.

He was standing over me, blank faced. He had a light pencil mustache running the course of his thin lips. His eyes were hard to make out in the gloom but I could've sworn there wasn't the slightest drop of white in them. Black as the night, they seemed.

"Wha—"

I think I floundered for the words for several moments. A stutterer stammering himself silent. The driver patiently waited until I had petered out.

"You're going to get up, walk back the way you came and forget what you saw," the driver said.

His face was flushed in green for a moment. There was a moan from the unit that stopped abruptly. The sound was like someone waking suddenly.

"Go," the man said.

I went.

•••

I don't remember seeing the limo leave. It must have though. When the sun finally blotted out the night, I made myself go back.

No one was there. The limo was gone. The unit shut up tight. Not the faintest reminder, aside from my terror-filled memories, of what had taken place there only a few hours before. I put my good ear against the damp metal door but didn't hear anything other than the pulse pounding in my head.

I knocked, quietly at first, then louder.

Then I remembered the keys in my pocket. The first one I tried didn't work. The second did. It turned noiselessly and lifted a quarter of an inch from the ground. I did my best to slow my breathing then yanked the door up.

It was empty.

•••

The shitty little door opened and Mr. Yellow waddled inside.

He slammed the door shut and set down the bag of fast food on the desk. He made to take off his jacket and froze when he saw me.

"Morning," Mr. Yellow said.

"Morning."

He took off his jacket and threw it behind the door.

I didn't move.

He plopped down onto one of the three little plastic chairs against the wall. He hung off both sides generously. He looked every bit the walrus balancing on a circus ball.

He opened the bag and started eating.

Call the police, he'd told me. Call the police.

"How was your first night," he said after some time.

Bits of hash brown clung loosely to his salt and pepper chin stubble.

He didn't look at me. Just kept right on stuffing fried potatoes and greasy biscuit into his glistening pink mouth.

"Interesting," I said.

Mr. Yellow's chomping paused and he shot me a sidelong look.

"Anything I need to know about?" he asked.

"I didn't call the police," I said.

He nodded and continued with his breakfast.

•••

Saturday night came on and I was back at the Stor-All. The weather had cleared during the day but clouds had come in with the twilight. Mr. Yellow gave me the keys without so much as a word.

I read "The Devil" and moved on to "The Kreutzer Sonata."

The night moved on toward morning. Just me and Leo. I smoked a pack of Winston Lights.

I waited for the limo to come again but didn't.

I did one round around the place in the quiet of the night, the sounds of the barges on the Maumee the only company I had besides my terrible memory. I didn't see or hear anything out of the ordinary.

•••

I didn't work again until Thursday night of the next week. Jimmy Clobs was in the office with Mr. Yellow. They were huddled over some papers and either didn't notice me come in or did not find it worth acknowledging.

"Evening," I said.

Mr. Yellow grunted a reply.

I sat down and listened to them talk. They were discussing knocking out one of the walls of the 10x10 units and combining it with another.

"Wouldn't it be cheaper to do two of the 10x5's?" Mr. Yellow asked.

"He needs the space. Long term too. Call Marty and get it done."

Mr. Yellow grunted his assent and Jimmy Clobs left without so much as a word to me.

"Who's the new client?" I asked.

Mr. Yellow didn't answer.

I repeated myself.

"Some guy. Wants more space than we got available right now," Mr. Yellow said.

"What's he storing?"

"That's none of our business, now is it?"

He shuffled the paperwork around on the desk, feigning some sense of order.

"See you in the morning," he said.

He cut out and I was left with Leo, nearly completed.

A sedan pulled up around three in the morning. A gloved hand emerged from the driver's side window and punched in the gate code. The car seemed to be rocking back and forth. The gate opened and the car disappeared inside.

"Here we go again," I told Maureen, the name I'd given the blonde on the back of the trailer door.

I stepped out into the early morning and lit a cigarette, a Misty Ultra Light. I opened the gate and crept through. I followed the smell of burnt oil, the sedan wasn't in good shape. I rounded a corner and watched as a man decked out completely in leather—leather vest, leather pants, leather wristlets and gloves, leather skull cap—open the trunk of his car. He stood a step back from the car as he opened it, making him look awkward, like the hug you give your middle-school girlfriend after a makeout session when you don't want her to know you've got a raging hardon.

The car shook and a leather-clad leg kicked out, followed by another. The legs swung wildly and the man took a quick step forward. His fists flew into the trunk like little leather lightning strikes. The legs stopped swinging and dropped limp, the right hanging out of the trunk.

The man wiped his fists on the back of his leather pants and they shone dully in the orange glow of the security lights. The man reached in and scooped up the person in the trunk. His body heaved with the effort.

What the—? My thought was interrupted by the immediate need to make myself scarce.

I jumped back around the corner and waited a slow count of five before peeking my head around it again.

The trunk stood open but the two leather people were nowhere in sight.

I took my steps slowly and as quietly as I could. I didn't hear anything. I looked into the open trunk but it was completely empty. I looked in through the windows of the car but it was empty too. Not so much as a gas receipt was to be seen. The car didn't have any license plates, not at the front or the rear.

Call the police. No. I don't know what I saw. It could've been anything. I need more information.

What an idiot I was.

"This doesn't concern you," a gruff voice said.

The man in leather stood huddled under the door of a unit. I hadn't even heard it open.

"What is going on here?" I asked.

I tried to muster all the authority I could in the voice, the voice of a security guard, and I'm not sure how successful I was.

"None of your concern," the man said.

His face was shaved very close to the skin but the skin was blue as the stubble began to sprout again. He wasn't wearing a shirt under the open leather vest and his chest was the hairiest I've ever seen. He could've been a gorilla.

He stepped out from under the unit's door.

"What is going on here?" I said.

I cringed at the raised octave and the quiver in my voice.

"It's time you leave," he said.

He turned back toward the unit. Inside, a man hung from the ceiling, suspended by his shoulders on thick metal hooks. His limp body spun slightly, like a windchime touched by the faintest of summer breezes.

The man slid the unit's door shut. His eyes burned into mine and he was out of sight.

•••

"This is Richard Dennison. I work at the Stor-All on South. I need someone here quick. I think someone is being murdered."

It took them twenty-five minutes to get there. One police car pulled up to the front office trailer. Its lights weren't even flashing. No siren blaring.

The cop left his cruiser running and stepped out to meet me.

"What's the problem?" he asked.

"I saw someone take a person from their trunk into one of the units."

His face was pure incredulity.

"You been drinking tonight?"

"No. Not at all," I said.

My face felt fit to burst.

"The man was hanging on some meat hook or something. We got to hurry," I said.

I opened the gate and the cop, seemingly unwillingly, followed me. I had to slow myself; he wasn't showing the faintest semblance of haste. He was walking the dog his kids wanted and promised to take care of but hadn't.

"What's your problem?" I asked.

Mistake.

"You better control yourself, son," he said.

He came to a complete stop.

"You better just calm the hell down," he said. "You on drugs?"

"No."

I started walking again. We turned the corner and the sedan was gone.

"The car was right here," I said.

I could still smell the burnt oil.

"You get the plate number?"

The officer opened his breast pocket and took hold of the little notebook he had nestled there.

"It didn't have any plates on it."

The cop left the notebook in his pocket and sighed.

"Which unit?"

"This one."

I put my ear to the door but didn't hear anything from inside.

"Open it."

I unlocked it and slid it up, prepared for horror. The man-chime cleaned to the meat, twirling on the hook. A butchery.

The room was empty.

My mouth hung open and the pulse beat in my temples.

This couldn't be, I thought. *I'd seen it. There had to be blood or something.*

The floor was clean. Not so much as a speck of dust.

"This some sort of joke?" the cop asked.

He stepped inside, ducking slightly under the lip of the door. He walked from one side to the other looking from the floor to the ceiling. Nothing hung from the ceiling. No hooks. No place for a hook to have been. Just the braces running parallel with the drive outside.

"No," I said. "I saw the man. He was all in leather and had another man in leather hanging from a hook right here."

"How long you been working here? They drug test you?"

The officer flicked his flashlight into life and directed it into my eyes.

•••

I sat behind the desk and couldn't bring myself to open the book. I sat there staring into nothing until Mr. Yellow came in at seven.

"Morning," he said.

I got up from the chair and made my way to the door. I had to side straddle the plastic chairs to let him pass. He smelled of stale sweat and onions.

I shut the door to the sound of the crinkling of the fast food bag.

•••

The cursor blinked, indented in the empty document. The words weren't coming. Again, the words weren't coming.

I couldn't focus. The man in leather. The green blob. The humiliating sobriety test.

What am I going to do? I'm worthless.

I slammed the laptop shut and went to the library.

•••

I read *At the Mountains of Madness* from start to finish. Lovecraft seemed like the only option. Leo wasn't fantastic enough. Not for the life I'd stumbled into.

The idea struck me as I returned the novella to the shelf. I could break down the wall by recounting the strange happenings of the Stor-All. I could rework them into a diary entry. Someone else working at a self-storage facility journaling the entire time.

Plus, it was the only income I contributed, a fact which Lucy reminded me of quite often.

•••

"Evening," I said.

Mr. Yellow grunted.

"Think I could pick up a few more hours?"

He paused.

"I'll have to check with Jimmy."

"Okay. Night," I said.

Mr. Yellow left.

I brought a green, spiral bound notebook and a pen. I opened it and started writing.

•••

The limo pulled up just before midnight. I couldn't believe my luck. I dropped to the floor and stole glances from between the blinds. I scoured the thing, looking for any detail worth noting. The windows were impossible to see through but I thought I saw a faint glow of green coming from the rear. I probably imagined it but scribbled it into the notebook anyway. The truth can't get in the way of a good story.

I let the limo pull through the gate and slipped out into the night to follow. I walked around the facility, deciding that coming from another direction would be the best option. Didn't want the driver to stop me from my observations.

The limo was idling, the brake lights much brighter than the security lamps high overhead. The unit door was standing open and the green glow spilled out into the night, mingling with the light from the brakes, looking like some demented Christmas decorations.

I clung to the shadows, careful not to be seen. I scribbled in my notebook and inched closer, trying to get a view of the inside of the unit.

There wasn't a way to see inside unless I stood where the limo parked. The driver would be watching.

Shit, I thought. I didn't want to meet the blob. I just wanted to see it. Watch it. Understand or at least learn enough to fabricate the rest. The block, "the wall" I'd taken to thinking of it as, loomed over me.

I retreated back around the corner to think.

Can't creep up on the limo. Far too dangerous. I want a story, not death. I could try the roof but I didn't think the height would give much of a view inside.

Headlights suddenly illuminated the fence behind me. I heard the closing of car doors followed by the limo lurching into motion. I bolted, running as fast as I could around to the other side of the unit building. I ducked into the space between the door and the building and made myself as thin as possible. The limo passed slowly but did not stop.

I crept around the corner to watch it through the gate before retracing my steps to the unit. It was empty. Not a thing to be seen now.

"Goddamn it," I said.

I opened the unit directly across from it, thinking I could wait in there behind a peephole for the limo to return another night. It was completely stuffed with furniture. There was barely enough room to close the door again.

So much for that.

I opened the unit to the left of the blob's. It was empty. The wall separating the two units, as well as the units on the other side of the building, was constructed of concrete blocks. I'd need a drill or something to make a peep hole. I scanned the roof and saw that concrete stopped some three feet under the wooden ceiling. I jumped, grabbed one of the support beams, and pulled myself up. There was a thin paneling there, much like the interior of a single wide.

I'd have to be waiting in here when the limo pulled up.

I didn't like the idea of sitting holed up in a storage unit for nights on end until the blob made its return.

The other side. Duh.

I walked around the building to the unit directly behind. It was empty.

I'll bring a drill tomorrow and make a small hole in the paneling, I decided.

•••

As soon as Mr. Yellow was gone, I grabbed the cordless drill from my car and drilled the little peep hole. I went back to the trailer and described my cunning plan in the green notebook.

I waited eagerly through the night, but nothing happened. I left disappointed when Mr. Yellow arrived at seven.

•••

Jimmy Clobs was there when I came in for the Sunday night shift.

"You wantin' some more hours?" he asked.

"Yessir," I said, closing the door and doing my best to avoid looking at Maureen and her lady lover.

"How many?"

"As many as you've got available, sir."

He nodded.

"Okay. Let's start with Tuesdays and Wednesdays along with the weekend shifts. We'll see how that goes and go from there."

"Thank you, sir."

He left and I described the interaction in the notebook.

The sedan came later that night. I was nodding off, my chin against my fist, when I saw it.

I kicked myself at not thinking of drilling a hole into the unit on the other side of the leather freak's.

The sedan pulled up to the gate and was put into park. The driver's door opened and the hairy man got out. He was decked out completely in leather again. He walked up to the trailer and opened the door.

I was shaking. I couldn't help it.

The man loomed there in the doorway for a moment, his eyes boring into mine.

"Mr. Dennison, do we have an understanding?" he asked.

"How do you know my name?"

He walked over to the desk, leaving the door standing open, but did not sit down in one of the shitty little plastic chairs. He leaned over the mess of the desk until his face was only inches from mine.

"You live over in the Heatherdowns Village. You frequent the library. You wrote seven published short stories in the past five years. Your wife, Lucy, a pretty little brunette, works at the nursing home down the street. Neither of you have family here."

I felt dizzy. Like I'd just run a mile holding my breath.

"Wha—"

I heard a muffled noise from his rocking car outside.

"Do we have an understanding, Mr. Dennison?"

The corners of the man's mouth lifted and his glaringly white teeth gleamed down at me.

"Yes, sir," I said.

He left. I watched him punch his code in and go about his business.

I was too shocked to follow. I noted the time.

1:15 a.m.

The sedan slowly pulled out of the facility at 1:55 a.m.

I held my breath until it pulled out onto South and headed away into empty streets. Then I opened the gate and made my way to the heather man's unit, drill in hand. I hesitated with the keys in my hand.

He could've boobytrapped it. He probably expects me to open it and see what he's left behind.

I strode around the building to the unit on the other side. I opened it and climbed around box after box of shrink-wrapped Beanie Babies to the back wall. I climbed up and drilled a small hole through the paneling.

It was too dark inside the other unit to see anything. I squinted and strained but saw nothing.

Just as I was getting ready to drop back down amongst the stuffed animals, the voice spoke.

"I thought we had an understanding."

Stunned, I flinched away from the sound of the leather man's rough voice emanating from the darkness and fell off my perch. The drill clattered beside me and snapped in two. I left it where it lay and scrambled to my feet. I slammed the unit shut and sprinted away toward the front office trailer.

He clotheslined me as I rounded the corner, hitting me in the throat and sending me crashing onto my back. All the air was beaten from my lungs and my throat worked but felt crushed. I floundered on the cracked pavement like a fish out of water.

"This will serve as your final warning," the leather man said.

He loomed into view over me, his face hard and pitiless.

"I cannot have you interfering in my affairs."

Air finally found its way into my lungs and I gasped.

"Wh-Wh-What . . . are . . . you?" I asked, breath coming in shuddering gulps.

"I will show you."

The man's hands were iron. They clasped onto my shoulders and lifted me effortlessly.

We walked back to the gate and exited. I turned up toward the trailer, assuming that's where we were heading, but the man's hard stare redirected me down the drive away from the Stor-All.

"Where are we going?" I asked.

He didn't answer. There wasn't a car in sight, streets empty at the late hour.

We walked around the block to an abandoned factory.

This isn't how I'm supposed to die, I thought. *This is a bad horror story. This isn't real life.*

We walked to the backside of the building, passed boarded up windows with spray painted declarations that the building didn't have any copper, to the parked sedan.

Those frantic, kicking legs replayed in my mind.

Shit. Shit.

"Come on, man," I pleaded. "I just got this job. I didn't know any better. I was just doing my job."

He opened the passenger side door for me.

I hesitated.

"Get in," he said.

I got in.

•••

We passed the SeaGate building at a crawl. The traffic lights blinked sleepily. Nothing moved.

"Where are we going?" I asked.

The man's leather gloves creaked as he adjusted his grip on the steering wheel.

The interior of the car smelled strongly of lemon-scented cleaning solution. The dashboard, though the car must've been an early nineties model, shone as if it were fresh off the lot. The seats, including the back, were completely covered in a thin, clear plastic lining so well installed I doubted it could be noticed until you sat down on it. The sweat from my ass and balls caught and pooled under me on the plastic.

"Where are you taking me?"

He turned onto Cherry then off onto a side road following the flow of the Maumee. Boarded up houses swam by in the closed passenger window, their plywood mouths gaping silent laughter at my circumstances.

A man lay on a bus stop bench asleep.

He pulled the car to the curb and left it running. He reached down beside the seat and popped the trunk. I saw it rise in the glow of the brake lights. The man got out of the car and slowly approached the sleeping man on the bench.

He hovered over him briefly. I swear he was listening to make sure the man was breathing and, with a speed I couldn't believe, he set about with a flurry of punches directed at the bench man's head. The struggle was brief due to the severity of the blows. Blood looked black in the night. The man ceased moving and the leather man scooped him up into his arms.

He had to walk by me on his way to the trunk. He stopped at my window for a moment and let his eyes beat down into mine. They shone with a frenzy that did not touch his face. They could've been black holes for all the gravity they had; I couldn't look away.

The unconscious man was deposited into the trunk and we headed back toward the Stor-All.

•••

He punched in the code and the gate slid open in jerks.

"It's gonna catch one of these days. Might want to get it looked at," the man said.

The car began rocking. For a split second, I thought a tire had blown. I could hear the man in the trunk's voice, quaking and raging, but couldn't make out any of the individual words.

"Why haven't you published anything of late, Mr. Dennison?"

The trunk popped as the man kicked and punched with everything he had in him.

I tried to answer him but nothing would come out.

The kicks and punches slowed into rhythmic pounding. He'd combined his efforts into single blows.

"I haven't been able to," I said.

"Well, here's you a story."

•••

He talked while he worked. He quieted the man in the trunk the same way he did the first time I saw him. The man must've been a boxer or prizefighter of some sort at one time or another.

He lifted the man from the trunk and dropped him onto the smooth concrete floor of the empty unit. He went back to the trunk and lifted the floor to space reserved for the sedan's spare. It wasn't there. In its place were two thick clamps with equally thick hooks, which came to needle point sharpness at the ends, sheets of plastic, and a selection of knives.

"Old family tradition," he said, removing the clamps.

He walked into the unit, stepped over the prostrate man, and, standing on his tippy toes, attached the clamps to the wooden ceiling braces. They had knobs on the side that he twisted to ensure an even tighter hold. The thin light of the single bulb in the unit flickered off the hooks as they settled near the man's shoulder.

"My dad taught me. His dad taught him. Ad infinitum," he said.

He retrieved the knives and the plastic from the trunk and let the flooring cover the space again.

He tossed them onto the ground in the back corner then lifted the unconscious man.

"You see," he said, the strain of lifting the man not showing in the slightest in his voice, "there is a quota that must be met."

He steadied the man on his shoulders and grabbed one of the hooks.

"Step inside and shut the door."

What else could I have done? I stepped inside and slid the door shut. The lone bulb gave the already small room a claustrophobic feel.

The man slid the hook under the man's left shoulder blade.

"Now that our understanding is finally understood," he said.

He let the man's weight fall onto the hook. Blood flooded out and the man woke with a cry.

"I can be of assistance to you in your time of need. You can help with the quota and things can continue in everybody's best interest."

The hanging man jerked on the hook but stilled himself almost immediately as the pain must've worsened with his efforts.

The leather man took the other hook and lifted the man by his underarm and let him drop, setting this hook the same as the first.

The hanging man didn't scream. The blood ran down his back, soaking through his shirt.

The man in leather spun on his heels and unfolded the plastic sheet under the hanging man just as the first drops of blood began to fall to the ground.

The man in leather picked up the thinnest of the knives and went back to the hanging man.

"You may want to sit down. Seeing for the first time can be overwhelming."

He slit the man's throat. Blood flowed from the smiling wound. The hanging man's eyes widened. His feet kicked. His hands tried to rise to his throat but the setting of the hooks prevented him.

I felt the ridges of the door as I slid to the floor. The room spun and the light seemed hazy. The last thing I saw was the man in leather standing over me, saying something. I couldn't make out his words.

•••

Mr. Yellow slammed the door shut, waking me. I shot bolt upright in the chair and saw that I was back in the office. I'd been asleep.

For one moment, I prayed it had all been a nightmare—but only for one moment. I knew what I had seen. What I had been a part of.

Mr. Yellow motioned for me to get up from the chair with his bag of fast food breakfast. I got up and found, surprisingly, that my legs were steady under me. I picked up my notebook and left.

•••

A quota. A fountain of blood. A tradition of spilling and ensuring. A noble but unenvious duty.

I wrote that morning like I had never written before. The words flashed across the screen faster than I could read. I was a man possessed.

•••

The limo pulled up to the gate and passed through. I threw down my notebook and stormed after it. I slipped by unnoticed to the other side of the building. I unlocked it, opened it just enough to slide underneath, and closed it gently behind me. The unit was in complete darkness. I couldn't see my hand inches from my face.

I listened as the unit on the other side of the building was opened. A green glow flooded through the hole I made near the roof. I glided toward it like a moth to flame. I climbed to the ceiling and craned my head until I could see in with my left eye.

The green was so vivid it took my eyes some time to adjust,

especially after being completely enshrouded in the complete darkness of the storage unit. As my eyes adjusted, I could make out general shapes of things. The limo tires just outside. The green blob pulsing and flashing. A woman on the floor, her tight skirt ruffled well past her upper thighs.

"Uhh," the woman moaned softly.

It could almost have been a sexual noise. Her head was disappearing as if it'd never been. The forehead. The eyes. The nose. Then the mouth and all was quiet.

The blob itself did not utter a sound. It flashed and glowed. Green swirled and intensified until the woman was gone.

I felt dizzy and sick. I had to hold on to the brace beside me to keep from falling to the floor.

The cloud seemed to sigh. It stopped swirling then began to settle. It seemed like it was a slow action but it was subtly quick. The green faded and became a woman. She was standing erect, chin upraised, and, thankfully, facing away from me. She was completely naked. Muscles corded her body and seemed to vibrate in their stillness.

I heard the opening of a car door and the driver stood before the opening to the unit. He held out a lush red coat open for the woman to step into. She held out her arms and let the driver clothe her. The coat hung well past her knees, nearly to her ankles. The driver opened the door to the back of the limo and she disappeared inside.

•••

I scribbled it down into the notebook and when I got home, I typed it all up.

•••

Friday
7 PM to 8 PM

5 **9** **12** GROWING FANGS (CC); 60 min.

The Halloween spirit haunts the Sever family home in this holiday spooktacular. Karol is becoming a woman but with mom, Margie, working graveyard shifts, it's up to dad, Jenson, to handle the situation. When Karol sprouts fangs and fur, dad learns that navigating womanhood might be more than he had bargained for.

7 WALNUTS—Cartoon

"It's the Better-Than-Average Squash, Corky Green." A perennial fall favorite for many generations. Corky Green and the rest of the Walnuts gang learn the true meaning of Halloween when Spoopy unearths human remains in Lewis's backyard. Meanwhile, Lewis battles fever dreams involving an overly large vegetable. (Repeat)

7:30 **3** **8** RALF (CC); 30 min.

RALF reminisces about Halloween customs on his home planet. Billie attempts to recreate the alien holiday here on Earth.

8 PM **83** MOVIE—Thriller; 2 hrs. ★★★

"Stor-All Self-Storage." (1985) An overnight job turns deadly for one security guard. A.S. Coomer, Colonel Sanders, Jim Varney.

EYEWITLESS NEWS AM
WITH ANDERSEN PRUNTY

WEEKDAYS BEGINNING AT 5:00 AM
ONLY ON WGHP CHANNEL 83

A blue pickup truck pulled up and passed through the gate. I hadn't seen it before. I finished the paragraph of the story I was proofreading, the blob and the girl, then followed it into the facility. It was parked in front of one of the closer unit buildings.

I didn't believe for a second I'd see something even remotely resembling normal but what I saw left me gaping.

Inside the storage unit a heavyset man clad only in a knife pleat cheerleading skirt was down on all fours with his ass back up to the far wall. Blowup sex dolls surrounded him. One was straddled on his back riding him. Another was hung from the ceiling on the back wall, a strap on sex toy fixed to the wall between its legs. The man was bumping himself back onto the toy violently.

The blowup dolls had been dressed up. Some were in cheerleader garb, others in basketball uniforms, but all were female. Blonde wigs hung from their heads at odd angles. Their mouths were all open 'O's with ruby red or sheer pink lipstick scrawled on their vinyl lips.

"What the—"

I hadn't meant to say it out loud.

The man stopped bouncing against the dildo and shot his head in my direction.

"Goddamn it," he said.

He slid off the toy, which jiggled moistly between the uniformed sex doll's legs. He lifted his fisted left hand and pointed it into the corner. A little beep sounded from where the man had pointed and only then did I notice the video camera on the tripod in the corner.

"What in the hell do you think you're doing?" the man asked.

His face was flushed with the effort he'd undertaken. There

wasn't the slightest glimpse of shame or embarrassment there.

"Sorry, I—"

"Damn right you're sorry. I pay rent here," the man said.

"Sorry, sir," I said. "I was just making sure everything was all right."

"Everything was all right until you showed up," the man said. "Now, I'm going to have to shoot the whole scene over again. I'm on a schedule, you prick. Jesus Christ."

•••

When I got back to the trailer, I laughed until I cried. Then I wrote it all down.

•••

I started sending off stories and some of them made it into the magazines. Some of them came back with personalized rejections: doesn't seem realistic; too fantastic; couldn't relate.

I laughed and laughed and laughed.

•••

The sedan pulled up and honked. I picked up my notebook and shut the trailer door. The man in leather waited until I was inside the car then punched in the gate code and pulled into the storage facility.

"There are dues that must be paid for our society to continue," he said.

The car shook and a muffled cry emanated from the trunk.

I couldn't make out all the words but I did recognize: God, help, please, and shit.

"This city, like all cities, is built on a foundation of blood and bone. Sweat makes it happen. There used to be more of us. Now there's only me."

He stopped the car outside his unit. We got out and walked around to the trunk.

Whoever was inside had sensed the car had ceased moving and fright must've froze them still as well.

"There's not much more I can do than what I already do," the man said.

He slid his key into the trunk and popped it open.

"No," a quaking voice hissed from inside.

I took a step forward and looked inside.

A wiry man was on his back, wide-eyed and panting. His thick glasses were askew and his tie had nearly come untied. He scurried deeper into the trunk and put out his hands and feet to ward away his captor.

"Please," he begged.

"There is a debt. Everything is built upon it. It must be paid."

He reached in and made to pull the wiry man out, but an animal instinct took over the captive and he kicked and flung his arms wildly.

The man in leather leaned back and waited until the other was still.

"There is no escape. You're serving a greater good."

"You're crazy."

The man in leather swung his arms suddenly, violently, and the man in the trunk ceased moving.

•••

He didn't ask for my help. He hoisted the unmoving man from the trunk, swung him up onto his broad shoulders, and put him into the unit. He went back to the trunk and got his tools.

"I'm old," he said. "We don't age the same way as you do. I've been doing this a long time."

He hung the clamps.

"I'm not sure how much longer I'll be able to continue. I will until I cannot."

He lifted the man and let the hook slip under his left shoulder blade. The man woke squealing.

"You must write the story. You must put it out there. If the spark lies unlit, somewhere maybe they will see, read, and understand."

He set the hook under the other shoulder blade. The wiry man's breath caught and he held his body rigid as if even the slightest motion caused a flurry of pain he couldn't begin to take.

The man in leather spread out the plastic under the hanging man.

"I'm not sure what will happen if the job isn't done. God help us."

He set to work.

I watched as long as I could, which probably wasn't too long, then slowly, quietly, slid the door shut and walked back to the trailer.

•••

I sent more of the stories off. They came back rejected.

Until one about the blob was picked up by an online horror magazine out of Australia. I printed the acceptance email and hung it on the wall above my desk.

•••

When I pulled into the little parking lot there were two pickups parked.

Gerald's Contracting & Construction, it read across both of their tailgates.

I opened the trailer's front door and there wasn't room for me to enter. Along with Jimmy Clobs and Mr. Yellow there were three other men in there. No one noticed me or at least did not acknowledge me standing in the open door.

"We'll knock out the wall tonight and should be able to finish up by the morning," one of the men was saying.

Jimmy Clobs was nodding his head, sending his triple chins into a violent wave of jiggling I couldn't look away from.

"As long as you don't get in anybody's way, you hear?" Jimmy Clobs said. "People pay us to be left alone with their shit. We're not trying to lose any business."

"Of course, of course. We'll be discreet. If anybody is in the area we can wait 'em out, Mr. Clobs."

"Expect a call from me in the morning," Jimmy Clobs said.

I stepped aside and let him pass down the four rickety stairs.

"Have a good night, Mr. Clobs," I said.

He didn't deign to answer.

"This is the night help," Mr. Yellow said, motioning his sausage fingers at me as I stepped into the trailer. "Anything goes wrong, he's your man."

With that, he too left.

•••

I punched in the code to the gate and let the two trucks pass through. I followed them to a unit building near the far east side of the premises. There were only three units in the entire building but they were the largest the facility had to offer. I opened the center unit and heaved the door open.

"Thanks, bub."

The men walked inside and went to the walls on each side.

"We'll start with this one," the man said.

I assumed he was Gerald, as he did all the talking thus far.

"Gerald. What exactly are you all going to do in here?" I asked.

I knew they were knocking down a wall to make the space bigger but I didn't want to go back to the front trailer yet.

Gerald turned slowly on his heels and gave me a sidelong glance before answering. I think he forgot I was even there before I spoke.

"Now, what's it matter to you . . . ?"

He let the *you* hang and it became two questions: what's it matter to me? and who was I?

"Richard Dennison," I said. "Just wondering."

"Well, do they pay you to wonder?"

I wanted to hit him. I didn't.

"You know where to find me if you need anything," I said.

I felt all three men's eyes on my back as I turned and walked away from the storage unit.

•••

An hour passed and one of the trucks pulled through the gate and headed west on South. The truck returned some time later with the bed weighed down until it nearly scraped the pavement. There were six metal and plexiglass tubes, roughly in the shape of coffins, standing in the back, tied together and bound to the bed.

The driver stopped at the gate and honked the horn four times.

I vaguely considered giving Gerald and his men the code to the gate then thought better of it. If Jimmy Clobs or Mr. Yellow hadn't given it to them then they sure as hell weren't getting it from me.

I stepped out of the trailer and casually lit a Misty Ultra Light. I inhaled deeply and blew the smoke out above my head before strolling over to the truck and leaning into the window. *Yes*, I thought, *I could get used to these.*

"Break time over, boys?" I asked.

The two men in the truck did not include Gerald.

"Open the gate, asshole," the driver said.

"Hey, hey," I said, lifting my hands up, palms out. "There's no need for that, now. I was just starting conversation."

"Open the gate."

I nodded and took another drag before punching in the numbers.

As the gate slid on its railing I said, "If you need anything, now, don't hesitate."

The driver didn't so much as look at me.

As the truck pulled by, I studied the contents of the bed. They looked like space pods or cryogenic chambers or something as ridiculous.

I went back to the trailer and scribbled away.

●●●

The truck passed through the gate again and returned with six more space pods. I let them through after another Misty Ultra Light. They didn't say one word to me. The night crept by without either of the trucks leaving. I decided to go and check up on how the work was progressing.

The closer I got to the storage unit the louder the sounds of the men working became. There was a clanging of metal on metal, which struck me as odd with the walls being concrete. I made my way around the corner of the building directly opposite and stayed away from the dim glow of the security lights. All three doors of the building were open and I could see the three men at work. They had knocked down both walls separating all three units so it was one long rectangular space with three sliding doors.

The space pods had been unloaded and were set in a row, twelve in all, some three feet apart from the wall of the first unit to the wall of the last. They were standing straight up and through their clear fiberglass tops I could see they were empty. They appeared to have headrests inside.

What in the world?

Gerald was bolting the last of the pods into place. One of the other men was setting up a small computer station with three monitors against the far wall, where the electrical socket was placed. The other man was fiddling with the backs of one of the pods.

I made my way back to the trailer without being seen.

•••

The trucks hadn't left when Mr. Yellow arrived. He dismissed me with a wave of his fast-food breakfast. I made to open the door but stopped.

"What are those men working on?" I asked.

Mr. Yellow shrugged his fat shoulders and plopped down onto the leather chair. It squeaked and I wondered vaguely how it could hold so much weight.

"Fuck if I know," Mr. Yellow said. "See you Wednesday, Dennison."

•••

"How's the job, Richie?"

"Boring," I lied.

I picked up the burger and took a bite big enough to puff out both of my cheeks.

"Well, at least it's something until you start picking up some more publication credits, right?"

I nodded my head. Cynthia was a dolt. I don't know what Lucy sees in her. I guess once you work with someone long enough professional camaraderie can eventually slip into friendship complacency.

"Luce, Mr. Stephens was an absolute wretch today," Cynthia said, turning to my wife. That was her nickname for my wife. It sounded like loose. "Pulled out his Foley and slung his piss at me and Wilma. I dodged it like the plague but poor Wilma."

More nursing home prattle. Always with the prattle.

I let my thoughts return to Gerald and his men and the weird pods they had installed.

What are they? What were they used for?

•••

On the way into work I passed by one of the newly installed "You'll Do Better In Toledo" signs that had popped up around the city.

I corrected the sign in my mind.

You'll Do Better To Avoid Toledo.

●●●

Mr. Yellow greeted me at the door.

"No rounds tonight," he said.

"What?"

"Don't make no rounds tonight."

"Okay . . . why?"

"That's what Jimmy says. No rounds tonight."

I nodded my head but couldn't wipe the confusion from my face.

"Look," Mr. Yellow said, "just sit in here all night and read your silly, little books. Take a nap. I don't care. Just don't go rounding. If anything happens—"

"Call the police, I know."

"Right. Night."

●●●

I sat behind the desk, my legs bouncing off the balls of my feet.

Don't round tonight.

My mom used to tell me not to scratch the bug bites or the poison ivy when I was younger but I couldn't help myself. As soon as she was out of sight, I dug my nails in deep.

I punched in the code and slipped through the gate. I stood listening after it closed again but heard nothing. I took the long way around the entire facility and moved only in the shadows. I took each step quietly and avoided all the loose gravel and trash.

I came around the corner to where Gerald and his pods had been and stood looking at the closed doors. There were no trucks there. No men working that I could see. I snuck over to each of the unit's doors and listened but heard nothing but the faint buzz of something electrical from within.

I pulled the keys from my pocket but found my hands shaking. I didn't open the door. Not then. I stood there with the breath caught in my throat and pussied out. I stuffed the keys back in my pocket and stalked back to the trailer.

•••

I tried to read but couldn't focus. I trained my eyes on the type and turned the pages but the stories remained unheard. All I could see was the standing pods. Images of what could fill them flashed through my mind. Little green men. Werewolves. Unconscious people.

What did the pods do?

I left the trailer to find out.

•••

I had my fingers on the keypad when the truck pulled up, Gerald's Contracting & Construction painted on the hood.

The horn honked and I moved aside so the driver could pull up to the gate. He rolled down the window and I saw that it was Gerald.

"No rounding tonight, sonny," he said.

I didn't know what to say.

"Open 'er up."

I punched in the code and the truck passed through. There were no pods in the back but two other men in the cab with Gerald.

I watched the truck's taillights round a corner to the rear then the gate slid shut.

I smoked a Misty Ultra and paced the length of the gate until it was gone.

Curiosity killed the cat, I thought.

Then images of strange cat-faced men howling mutely behind the plexiglass flourished in my head.

"Goddamn it," I said and punched in the code.

•••

The doors were closed but both of Gerald's trucks were parked in front of the storage unit. The buzzing from within was louder. There were other noises too. Strange noises: the banging of metal on metal; tiny whimpers that shouldn't have been audible but seemed somehow amplified; a terse foreign tongue barking some strange sounding language I couldn't place.

I crept closer, taking each step as if on a tightrope. The closer I got, the more confused by the speaker from within I became. It didn't sound like any language I'd heard before. I mean, Toledo isn't the most diverse place on God's green earth but it's not exactly vanilla either.

I put my hands on the farthest door to the left. It seemed to hum with some electrical impulse. It didn't shock me exactly but as I placed my hands on it, I felt the hair on the back of my neck and arms stand on end.

What the . . .

I put my ear to the door and all of the sounds stopped.

I jerked my head back as if I'd been slapped.

I stepped back, made to run. I thought I'd been heard or felt, detected somehow, as if I'd disturbed the energy emanating from within.

Then all the air around me surged forward toward the unit. It was as if some great beast suddenly woke from its slumber with a start.

I was balanced precariously on my left foot, moving to take a step back when it happened. I was pulled forward and stumbled, catching myself with my hands with a thump against the door. That time I was shocked by the door. My hands buzzed with the charge. It wasn't the usual pop and jolt of touching an electric fence. This was a hum and pull like a great unseen body of water, a drafting ocean's consuming undertow. My body was swept from the pavement and pressed against the door as if by magnet.

My eyes filled with tears and the insides of my nostrils prickled like I had to sneeze the worst sneeze of my life.

I pushed back with everything I had but couldn't break free. I hung there like a bug in a zapper, helpless.

Then, all at once, it stopped. I slid off the door into a heap on the pavement. My arms and legs felt heavy, thick and wooden. It took me some time to regain use of them. I rose on unsteady legs and wobbled away from the unit.

•••

It took me the rest of the night to recover the comfort and ease of my body.

This must be what it's like learning how to walk again, I thought.

Mr. Yellow came with the morning but the trucks remained inside the facility. I checked my watch walking down the stairs and nearly stumbled when I saw the little metal hands bend forward, their points dug deep into the watch face. Tiny spiderwebs of cracks spiraled away from where they touched like the broken surface of a clear lake.

•••

The next night I watched as a red pickup passed through the gate. About an hour later a man on foot emerged from inside the facility and knocked on the trailer's door. Maureen's hair seemed to blow in the wind with the pounding from the other side.

"Come in," I shouted.

The door opened and the man came in. His face was creased with a frown.

"I don't know how but I backed into the building," he said.

"What?"

"Come on," he said, leaving the door open for me to follow.

The man had pulled into his unit, one directly across from the space pod building. The rear end of his truck was crunched into the middle door of the space pod building.

"How the hell?"

"I don't know. I came to change my oil and serpentine belt and when I finished it was like someone had smashed in the pedal and I couldn't get the truck to stop."

I walked into the man's unit. There was a little puddle of oil near the front, surrounded by a plethora of tools and toolboxes. The man used his unit as his garage.

I followed the path of his truck from his unit across the pavement. There were burnt tire tracks all the way. The man had locked the brakes trying to stop but it hadn't done any good.

We went back to the trailer and called for the police to make an accident report.

•••

A strange thing happened when the officer, young and fresh out of the academy, was busy with the paperwork. There was another suck of the air around the space pod unit, much weaker than the night before, then the security lights dimmed and the police cruiser's lights blinked and the siren began a wail but stifled it like a yawn.

All three of us, the driver of the truck, the police officer, and myself, looked up and paused but did not comment.

•••

A couple of hours later the lights in the trailer blinked and nearly went out. The hum of the fan slowed but the pause was so brief the fan did not have time to stop spinning completely before it picked back up.

Something weird's going on with those space pods.

Another two hours passed and one of Gerald's trucks pulled up to the gate and honked. This one had a truck topper covering the bed. There were no windows on it and I could not see what the truck was carrying, if it was carrying anything at all.

I opened the door, went to the window and peered in. Gerald was behind the wheel.

"Open the gate," he said.

I lit a Misty and inhaled deeply. I shuddered, fighting back a cough.

"Open the gate, asshole," he said.

"What's in the space pods?"

"What?"

"The space pods you've got in the unit. What's in 'em?"

"None of your damn business. Open the gate."

We stared at each other through squinted eyes. Then I sighed and punched in the code.

The first hint of the morning sun was blanching the sky over the Maumee. I made to check the time on my watch and stared at my naked wrist for several seconds before remembering that the pods had killed the thing.

Shit, I thought.

•••

I didn't work again until Wednesday. I got there just at dusk, the security lights tinkling into life throughout Stor-All.

It wasn't thirty minutes into my shift when the power faltered. This time the fan had time to stop completely before resuming its spinning.

"That's it," I said to myself. "Time to figure this shit out."

As I made to open the door the truck with the topper pulled up.

"Great."

I went through my process of making Gerald wait, smoking my cigarette all the way down to the filter before approaching the window and letting him in.

"What's in the back?" I asked.

Gerald jerked his head around. I followed the truck through the gate at a trot and changed to a stroll, doing my best not to show how winded the short jog had made me, as he was stepping out onto the pavement.

"What are you doing here?"

"Making my rounds," I said, lighting another Misty. "You know, being security and all."

He didn't shut the driver's side door right away. He looked at me then at the truck topper like he was calculating something in his head.

He shut the door and said, "None of your business. Make your rounds."

He leaned against the truck and folded his arms.

There was nothing to do but go. It felt like my tail was between my legs but I made sure not to show that he'd won. I sauntered by as if that's what I had planned to do all along.

I circled back around and approached from the way I had come. Gerald was waiting for me, leaning against the side of the building, all but hidden in the shadows.

I jumped and felt my face flush red when he spoke.

"Are we going to have a problem?" he asked.

I didn't reply.

"Am I going to have to tell Mr. Clobs that you're harassing a paying customer?"

"No, sir," I said.

I spun on my heels and trudged back to the trailer.

The truck left some short time later.

It wasn't an hour and a half before it returned though.

I opened the gate for him without so much as a word passing between us. Just as the gate was starting to close, it staggered and stopped. The security lights blinked off. Gerald's truck's lights and engines cut out. The truck kept moving as if pulled. It drifted on toward the back of the facility for some fifteen seconds or so then, all at once, all the power returned. The security lights glowed back to life. The taillights of the truck burned red and the gate shuddered forward and closed.

•••

The truck left then returned within two hours. This continued until the sun rose and I left.

•••

"What's with that Gerald guy and that back unit?"

Mr. Yellow harrumphed.

"I thought they were just gonna knock down a wall to make the place bigger," I said. "Seems like they've been at it for quite some time."

"So?"

"Just wondering."

He left and the night came. The power surged, stronger and longer in duration than before. Gerald's truck pulled up, the one with the covered bed, and I let him through.

He left and within two hours returned again. This happened throughout the night until the morning arrived and Mr. Yellow relieved me.

"Why don't you give Gerald the code for the gate?" I asked.

"If Jimmy wanted to, he would have," Mr. Yellow said.

Fair enough, I thought.

I went home and wrote a story about the space pods. In it, the truck was bringing imprisoned aliens to the unit for rehabilitation. Their ship had crashed somewhere in Lake Erie and a coalition of alien lovers broke them out of a secret government prison. They were nursing the little green men back to health and sending distress signals to their people some many light years away.

•••

I watched for more clues the next night. The power surges seemed to be growing stronger and stronger. Gerald's schedule seemed to be to come and go every two hours.

Weird, I thought as I scribbled it all down into my notebook.

I found myself watching the sky every time I stepped out to smoke a Misty.

Flying saucers and little green men. *What sort of writing hack had I become?* I wondered.

Gerald pulled up and I let him through.

•••

I finished the story about the heroics of the alien rescuers and sent it off. Bradley Kubrick was the protagonist and as a reward for his service he was taken away to live forever with those he risked his life for.

It was rejected by twelve of the thirteen science fiction magazines I shopped it to. The thirteenth was an online only magazine, but it was another credit on the ol' CV.

•••

The limo glided up and entered.

I don't know where I had been. Somewhere near the middle of *A Confederacy of Dunces*. I saw the flash of the brake lights. I let the book fall to the desk and hurried to follow it.

I made it into my secret spying unit as the first glows of green burst through my peephole. I climbed up and watched.

The blob had a brunette in a skimpy cocktail dress on the floor.

Her head was being enveloped. She moaned and whimpered slightly, a near sexual sound. Her eyes were expressionless and her mouth was open in a pout. Her lips were ruby red with lipstick and her toe and fingernails matched.

I watched as the woman's face dissolved into the greenery. Half-way down her long, slender neck the small bulb above the monster and its prey flashed and then faded into darkness. I felt a pull in the air and my face was pressed into the peephole against my will. The blob and the woman and the limo outside were all pulled several inches eastward toward the space pod unit.

"What in the hell," a woman's voice within the green blob shouted.

The suction surged once, twice, then resolved to stillness. The light above the blob blinked back on. The limo driver emerged in the foot of the door looking wide-eyed.

"Did you feel that, madame?"

"Of course I felt it, you idiot," the blob spat. "What was it?"

"I do not know, madame."

"Well, go find out!"

The driver turned and fled from sight.

The green blob seemed to fade a bit and the brunette's body fell limply to the cement.

"Fucking hell," the blob said.

Bits of a pale woman smeared and stretched appeared in the green mist. The green intensified until the anatomy of the woman elongated and returned to a solid green. The brunette was lifted into the air and the blob resumed its meal.

I climbed down from my perch and quietly left the unit. I snuck around the corner of the building, trying to dart looks in all directions at once, and made my way toward the space pod unit. As I was crossing the main drive, which led to the gate and the trailer, I saw the leather man's sedan driving through.

Sweet Jesus, I thought. *All the freaks are here at the same time.*

I stood there in the middle of the drive and let the headlights grow until the car stopped at my feet.

The man in leather got out and stood looking at me, doe-eyed in the lights.

"What is wrong, Mr. Dennison?" he asked.

"Now is not the best time for you to be here."

"I have to do my duty."

I swallowed and nodded my head.

How do you argue with a sadistic serial murderer? Answer: you don't.

•••

He retrieved the hefty man from the trunk. The man had to weigh 250. He was out cold. The man in leather lifted him with only the slightest strain. The cords of muscles leaped but his breath remained steady.

"The quota must be met."

I nodded my head.

Of course, the quota had to be met. Worry not about the people-eating green blob or the weirdness coming from the space pods.

He let the man drop to the floor and set up his hooks.

"There will come a time, sometime very soon, I think," he said, setting the hooks into the man's back, "where this will be a thing forgotten. As I said, I think I am the last."

The fat man woke with bulging eyes. Spit flew from his mouth as well as a yowl any street cat would shed one of its lives for.

The man in leather set the other hook then spread out the plastic.

"It is imperative you write my story, Mr. Dennison."

The fat man held his breath like a child going through a tunnel or over a bridge, as if he thought the pain would relent if he stopped breathing. I guess he was right, kind of.

A scream tore through the night from somewhere outside that unit. The leather man and I stood staring at each other. All was quiet then except for the steady drip-drop of the fat man's blood.

"What's going on, Mr. Dennison?"

"I have no clue."

The man in leather turned to the fat man and slit his throat with a speed and lack of hesitancy that made my head spin. It was some-thing akin to taking out the garbage. Something that required no thought, no emotion, nothing other than the flick of the wrist and a split second.

We stepped out and stood listening.

"Dennis?" a woman's voice called. "Dennis?"

I recognized it but it took me a moment in my muddled state to place it with the woman that was the green blob.

"Shit," I said.

I made to move back inside the unit but she rounded the corner of the building and saw us.

"Where is my driver?" she shouted.

She stood, stark naked, some twenty yards away at the end of the building.

"What have you done with Dennis? He better be unharmed."

"Who's Dennis?" the man in leather asked me.

"Her driver," I whispered.

"Who is she?"

"You don't want to know."

She put her hands on her bare hips. Her legs were a shoulder's length apart.

"You don't want to make me angry," she said.

Images of the Hulk, Banner's transformation, flashed in my head and I couldn't help but smile. I loved that shit when I was a kid.

The man in leather turned around and looked at the dead man in his unit.

"I don't think we have your Dennis," he said.

The woman stared at us, hard, then stomped away eastward. Her bare feet made a smacking sound on the pavement.

"I think you should go, Mr. Dennison."

I nodded and went.

•••

"Miss," I called. "Miss."

No answer.

I walked toward the space pod unit, looking down each lane between the buildings. The place was empty, it seemed.

"Miss."

I came to the last building. The middle door was open. The green light pulsed from within. It was a short walk that seemed to take a long time. I held my breath and peeked inside.

The blaring of the horn caught me completely off guard. I leapt back and knocked my head against the cement wall of the building.

I collapsed to my knees and held my head. Bright lights blinded me and the world spun. The last thing I saw was Gerald running past me and through the door of the storage unit.

•••

"Sleeping on the job is a good way to get your ass canned."

My eyes, crusted and heavy, opened and Mr. Yellow's ugly face slowly came into focus.

I tried to shake my head, but a wave of nausea swept over me and I stilled myself.

"Wh—?"

That was all I could manage. It felt like there was an angry hive of bees swarming between my ears. I could feel the pulse in my temples, beating like a gong.

"Jesus, kid," Mr. Yellow said. "Go home."

•••

"Have you noticed anything weird?" I asked.

Mr. Yellow rose from the leather chair.

"What?"

"Weird, you know? Like out of the ordinary?"

"Are you high?" Mr. Yellow asked.

I think it was more of a rhetorical question.

"No."

He grunted and made for the door.

"Seriously," I said, grabbing his sweaty forearm.

He looked down at my hand then into my eyes. He looked pissed. I let go of his arm.

"Like any power outages or anything like that?"

"No."

He narrowed his eyes and studied my face.

"Is there anything you need to tell me?" he asked.

I think there's a fucked up science experiment involving aliens in one of the units. A leather fetishist serial killer in another. Oh yeah, and a beautiful woman that transforms into a people eating green blob.

I shook my head, thinking maybe I *was* high. Or maybe losing my mind.

"Try and stay awake tonight," Mr. Yellow said. "If you can manage it."

•••

I went through the gate as soon as Mr. Yellow was out of sight. I walked down each of the lanes between the unit buildings, but the place was empty. Dusk hung in the air like it was doing everything it could to stave off the night. The security lights blinked on and glowed weakly.

I made my way to the space pod building just as the night won out. The sky was dark, not a star to be seen in Toledo's light pollution. I kept my distance from the units, standing some ten feet away and just looking at them, waiting.

I felt the air still then surge forward. The security lights flashed then went out. I stumbled forward but leaned back with all of my weight.

I must look like one of those Weather Channel reporters in a hurricane, I thought.

The pull stopped and I fell backwards onto my ass on the hard pavement.

The doors of the unit building began to tremble then shake.

"What the—"

The doors jerked upward and, from the darkness within, twelve pale shapes emerged. They were man-like—two legs, two arms, a head—but that's where the similarities ended. They were completely devoid of color, nearly transparent. Their bodies were nearly feature-less. They had no eyes, no noses, no ears, no body hair. They had long pale fingernails, more claws than nails, really. In the middle of their faces was a circular hole.

Assholes?

They definitely looked every bit the sphincter.

They stepped out on the pavement on toe-less feet.

All of the hair on my body stood and leaned toward them like a shaded plant reaching for the sun. My body felt leaden, heavy. My arms lifted without my command and extended toward the creatures.

What is happening?

They moved slowly but steadily forward, toward me.

I could not move on my own accord. It was terrifying.

Their asshole mouths began to open as they closed in on me. They were completely lined with nearly translucent teeth, like those on a gar but in the mouth of a lamprey.

Somewhere to my right, I heard the high whine of an engine. All twelve of the creatures stopped and turned their asshole faces toward the sound.

The leather man's sedan mowed through the crowd, sending some of them flying through the air, some thumping under the wheels.

One smashed into the unit building beside me and went limp on the pavement not three feet away. Its smell was overwhelming. It was a mixture of something strangely earthly, like freshly tilled cemetery dirt, and something wholly chemical. It made my eyes water.

The sedan came screeching to a halt and the man in leather stuck his head from the open window.

"Get in, Mr. Dennison."

I found I had control of my body again and got into the car.

•••

"They are electromagnetic vampires," the man in leather said.

"What?"

"They feed on human blood. They render their victims paralyzed through a blast of electromagnetic currents."

I think I am high. Or highly insane, I thought.

He whipped the car around the corner of one of the unit buildings and sped toward the gate.

"How?"

"Gerald Finch Godwin."

He locked the brakes in time to avoid slamming into the slowly opening gate.

"The contracting guy?"

"The very same."

The car hurtled through the gate, out of the parking lot and onto

South Ave.

"Where are we going?"

•••

His leather gloves were fingerless. His hands continuously tightened then loosened then doubled his grip on the steering wheel. The streets were empty. The traffic lights blinked their signals but the man in leather did not heed them. He blasted through a red light on Adams and the car was briefly flashed by the traffic cam.

"You just got a ticket," I said.

"No plates," he said.

I smiled. I hated those goddamn traffic cams and I couldn't help but feel good at being able to stick it to them for once, even if it was vicariously through the driving of a psychopath.

"Who are you?" I asked.

He let his eyes drift in my direction but did not answer.

The city blurred by in the window and we rode in silence.

•••

The highway turned and crossed the dark and quiet Maumee. The casino blurred by and the man in leather took an exit. I'd never been to this part of the city. Never had a reason to. I wasn't a laborer, didn't work on the refinery or the barges.

The sedan moved swiftly through the empty streets, swerving to miss the crater-sized potholes.

"If you want me to write your story, I need to know more about you."

The man in leather smiled. It was not a pleasant thing.

"I'm not from around here," he said.

I thought of the space pods and the alien like creatures. It dawned on me they were vampires. Real life vampires.

What the fuck, Toledo?

"Where are you from?"

"It's not really important. I was born twice."

I twisted under the seat belt to get a better look at him.

He pulled the car into a parking lot in front of what the city would call a "blighted" warehouse. He cut the engine and sat staring straight ahead with his gloved hands in his leather-clad lap.

"First to my mother. Secondly to man," he said. "I am a servant of man, you see. I am one, probably the last living member, of the Order. We keep it all moving. The world is made of blood and fueled by blood."

I believed him. I just saw electromagnetic vampires. I saw a green blob that feasts on women. I wouldn't have been surprised to know the world is actually a living, breathing creature that also fed on men and women.

"Are you talking about the world or just Toledo?" I asked.

He looked at me fully then.

"Does it really matter?" he asked. "If it were just Toledo, is that such a small thing to lose? It would spread from here."

I nodded but didn't really understand.

"You don't have it in you or I'd make you successor. You're weak in that respect, Mr. Dennison."

This shamed me and my face flushed. A mass murderer informing me that I didn't have the grit to do what he did. Somewhere in the back of my head I understood the absurdity of that but it was somewhere really, really, really far back there.

"I could try," I said.

I tried to imagine myself, leather clad, lifting some warm, unmoving person up off the cold cement floor of a storage unit and hanging them by their flesh on suspended hooks. I tried to imagine using the collection of knives the man kept. I tried to imagine rending the flesh meat and the whole into parts.

I couldn't.

"Don't be ashamed," he said. "We all have our stations. I was destined to keep it all running. You were destined to tell my story. Whether or not it all continues is destined to be seen. Perhaps the Order is destined to starve off and a new Order will take its place."

He opened the door and got out. I followed.

The night felt chillier than it should've been, at least that's how it seemed to me. Maybe it was a mental quavering from seeing so much weirdness.

Unholy Toledo, I remember thinking. *Unholy Toledo. Holy Toledo. Wholly Toledo.*

The door to the warehouse stood open. Darkness yawned out from within.

The man in leather who had been born two times did not hesitate. He walked into the darkness as if it were another form of light, which I guess it was.

I looked around before following him. There wasn't anything moving. Nobody near. What shreds of rationality remained in me told me the man was a killer and we were alone, therefore, I was in danger.

The other part of me I have since dubbed as Wholly Toledoan reminded me the man could have killed me at least a dozen times since I'd discovered him. In all probability, a hundred times moreover, since he seemed to know all about me before I even learned of his existence.

I followed the man into the darkness.

•••

"Here."

I couldn't see anything. I took hesitant, careful steps toward the voice.

"You are almost there."

The voice didn't sound nearer. It didn't sound as if I had made any progress toward it at all.

"Do not be afraid."

I trembled.

My right foot bumped into something hard. I reached out and felt the wall. It was smooth, too smooth to be the wall of some abandoned warehouse. It felt polished and luxurious; the gilded wall of a palace.

"And then there was light."

The man in leather scratched a match into life. The hollow cheeks stood in stark contrast to his full beard. His eyes glittered in the dancing flame. He leaned forward and lit a candle then dropped the match, letting it burn itself out on the floor.

"This is where I was born for the second time, Mr. Dennison."

He lifted the candle, which I saw was in an ornate holder carved into some intricate shape I couldn't quite place in the dim lighting, and lit several more just above where my hands had felt. The place began to take shape. The walls gleamed golden in the shaking light. The floor ascended by a row of steps stretching out beyond the candles' luminance.

"This is where I will make my final testament, be absolved of my failures, reap what I have sown and pass from this plane."

His face turned from mine and he walked up the stairs. There were nine of them. At the top was a stage of sorts, a pulpit is perhaps the better term.

He turned up there and lifted his chin. His eyes were covered in the shadows of his beard and cheeks. He looked eyeless.

I suddenly felt surrounded by hundreds of unseen spirits. The place felt claustrophobic, oppressive, mass attendants in St. Peter's Square tight. Ghosts upon ghosts upon ghosts.

I stared up at the man and he looked every bit the Old Testament character. The leather clothing looked less hard rock gay and more skin of my enemies tough.

"I was brought here, taken from the ones that birthed me. I was given the choice to return to the world outside or enter the world of the ancient machine. The Beast, we call it."

That's what it is, I thought. *Not surrounded by ghosts but in the den of some giant sleeping monster.*

"You see and you don't see. There are monsters visible and monsters hidden. The Beast requires blood to keep the hidden hidden."

Green blobs. Electromagnetic vampires. What else was out there?

"We are at the end of the line. The Beast stirs, grows unsatisfied.

The Order has failed."

Maybe the Beast's eyes were slitted. Maybe it was feigning sleep.

I backed away from the stairs, retreating into the darkness.

"You can call me Om. The lullaby of the Beast."

•••

The truck pulled into the parking lot and Gerald Finch Godwin stepped out. He opened the door of the trailer and stood there.

"We need to talk," he said.

We did.

"There is something in that unit that you don't understand. Couldn't possibly understand. Don't need to understand," he said. "You understand?"

I nodded but he continued.

"Those . . . creatures are essential. They are harvesters," Gerald said.

"Harvesters?"

"The world runs on blood," he said.

How was this something I hadn't known until so recently? The very fundamental cause of perpetuation.

I blinked like a schoolkid.

"I've been feeding them," he said.

The covered bed of the pickup truck.

"Nobody special," he said, quickly.

I guess he thought I was going to argue that everyone had worth, so he hurried on.

"No one that civilization needs. Not the important ones. Just drifters and throwaways. They have grown much quicker than I had anticipated. They are old enough to hunt for themselves. They feel compelled to."

"The power surges?"

"Feed. 7,665 seconds is 2.1291 hours," he said.

"What?"

"The seventh letter, the sixth twice then the fifth. Seven, six, six, five. Feed."

We stared at each other in silence. I didn't know what to say.

"What are they?" I asked, finally.

"The Order has died but the quota must be met. I made them. They are ones and zeros and skin and bones. The Beast will be fed. Do not interfere."

Gerald Finch Godwin turned on his heels and left the door open.

•••

I wrote Om's story. I sent it off. It came back in my stamped, self-addressed envelopes. I reworked it, adding in an imperative under-current of bloodthirst, and sent it off again.

•••

The limo did not return. I wondered if the blob had died. I didn't know how I felt about it.

The weeks passed with the power surges and the screams in the night. I did not make rounds. I did not leave the trailer. Gerald stopped coming, the Harvesters could feed themselves.

•••

On a Wednesday, just before heading off to the Stor-All, I got a let-ter. It was from a little magazine called *Horror of Horrors*. They ac-cepted Om's story. It would be published on their website and in their tabloid-style magazine.

I brought the letter to work with me, hoping to show him. He did not return either.

I'm not sure what that story has caused. I'm not sure anybody read it. I was paid in copies of the magazine and I went out to every bookstore I could find in Toledo, Ann Arbor, and Detroit but couldn't find a copy of it on the shelves. The other stories in the magazine were just as strange as my own. They all were fantastic and dark; worlds of bloody requirements and sacrifices. A letter to the Editor on the magazine's last page read:

All will be well. The Harvest has come.

-O.M.

PRIMITIVE

LUCAS MANGUM

For Galloway

EDITOR'S NOTE

THE PAGES THAT FOLLOW WERE _found among the belongings of a Professor Walton Roberts, who disappeared somewhere in the Tatoosh Wilderness near the town of Paradise, Washington, along with his three companions: programmer Bryan Hobbs; professional mover Hank Sullivan; and corporate banker Tony Tabs. Along with these papers, authorities discovered remains of an illegal campsite, and an RV registered to Tabs was found abandoned on the outskirts of Paradise. Additionally, evidence suggests the missing men may have engaged in the illicit killings of several wolves in the area. As of this writing, no other trace of these four men has been uncovered. It has also been speculated their disappearance is somehow tied to a series of nearby child murders and the vanishing of a Ms. Luca Barath, whose own son was a suspect in the killings. However, no evidence linking these tragedies has ever been found._

MOON MOUNTAIN

WE LOADED UP TONY'S RV on Thursday evening. It was Memorial Day weekend. The semester was over, Tony and Bryan had taken off from their jobs, and Hank had been laid off again. The stars had aligned perfectly. I had five whole days away from it all. Five days with my high school buddies. Men I hadn't seen in almost fifteen years. For most of those fifteen years, we talked about doing something like this, but nothing materialized until now. It couldn't have come at a better time either. Not for me, anyway.

I'd just lost custody of my son, Wiley. Apparently, my ex-wife and the judge she was fucking determined my drinking was a detriment to my parenting. Never mind I only drank at night. Never mind I didn't black out. Never mind I still held down my tenured position at California State University's Department of History. Of course, Ayla was a good lay. That probably had some bearing on the Honorable Alexander Smart's ruling. Not that I could prove anything was going on. Anyway, I planned to get my son back, but first, I needed some time away. Four nights in the Tatoosh Range should do the trick.

As we packed the RV with supplies, Tony's wife made barbecue short ribs and mashed potatoes. His twin daughters chased the family German shepherd around the expansive front lawn. The sun was setting too fast, but I tried not to think about it. We hadn't planned this trip so I could worry about time.

When we finished, the seven of us sat down to one of the best meals I'd had in years. I felt like a man who'd just gotten out of prison. It took all I had not to devour the food in an embarrassingly short amount of time. Ayla was a shit cook, not like Tony's wife, Yvette, at all. That wasn't the only way they differed. Ayla had small tits and practically no ass. She was pasty-faced, and her hair was damaged from frequent dyeing. Yvette, on the other hand, was thick where it counted, dark-skinned, and her hair was a nest of sensuous braids.

Tony Tabs had a good life. Though he had grown up in the same low-income cesspool as the rest of us, he'd turned out okay. He was Vice President of Corporate Banking at a Sacramento financial institution. He had a house in El Dorado Hills, two beautiful twin girls, and an obedient but intimidating dog. Plus, he got to nail Yvette whenever he wanted. I wasn't jealous of him or anything, but sometimes I wished my life was as sweet. It was nice of him to share the wealth this weekend.

After dinner, Tony and Yvette put the girls to bed while Bryan, Hank, and I sat on the back deck drinking High West Campfire

Whiskey. Bryan did most of the talking. Found out after college he was into dicks, which was fine, long as he didn't touch mine. One high school experience aside, I just wasn't into gay shit.

On this night, while Hank and I watched the stars and moon come out, Bryan went on about how welcoming the tech world was to people like him. He talked about his three cats: an orange tabby named Eva; a gray and white domestic shorthair named Jack; and Oliver, who looked like he was crossbred with a skunk in all his pictures. He said he wasn't dating anyone seriously, but was still having fun, and not exactly ready to settle down. I nodded here and there and told him that was good. Hank didn't say shit. I always thought he might be a bit homophobic. Just a bit though. I mean, he wouldn't have stayed friends with us if it bothered him that much. Of course, maybe he had nothing against gay men at all. Maybe he was just quiet because, like me, he was also recently divorced and having no fun being single, whereas Bryan seemed to be enjoying himself. Either way, I think we were all ready to hit the road.

Tony came outside with a big grin on his face.

"You guys save enough Campfire for me?"

"Sure, man, you gotta glass?" Hank asked and proffered the bottle.

Tony waved it away. "Kidding. Since it's my rig, I'll drive first. Give you guys a chance to sober up."

"I'm sober," Bryan said. "Perfectly sober."

"With you I could never tell," Tony said. "You've only ever had one gear."

"I can drive if you need me to," Bryan said.

"Nah, I'd rather start us out." Tony opened his palm to show us the keys. "Finish those shots, boys. We got a lot of miles ahead."

Tony went inside. Hank grimaced as he knocked back the remnants of his booze. I held my nose and did the same. Bryan had no trouble putting the rest of the whiskey down. He slammed his glass on the nearest tabletop and nodded. We all got up and followed Tony through the house. At the front door, Yvette hugged all of us. She lingered on me and told me to take care of Tony. I told her I would and then she released me and gave Tony a goodbye kiss. I tried not to stare, but the slurp of their tongues was hard to ignore.

Hank sat up front with Tony. Bryan lay down on one of the RV's built-in beds. I sat all the way in the back to try writing something. I'd told myself I'd get some writing done on this trip. Unfortunately, I had no idea where to start. It'd been a while since I'd written fiction. I couldn't even remember the last time I'd tried. Though I still sometimes called myself a novelist, I'd only published one book when I was in my mid-twenties. A mystery novel called *The Hangman's Gambit*. It'd done okay, but not good enough to launch my career. Turned out I was better suited for academics.

Still, there's something inside me that yearned for release. Could be another book. But sometimes it felt more primal than that, like inside of me lay a dormant monster caged by modern society, more specifically, caged by me, who was deceived by modern society's perceived treasures. I sometimes thought maybe this same sleeping hunger dwells in all of us, but Tony seems pretty content, Bryan too. Even Hank, through simplification forced upon him by poverty, might have it figured out. Could be they're lying. That's always possible. Could also be they're still riding a high and haven't come down yet. Either way, they're different from me. I'm aware of this monster. Sometimes I'm so aware, I feel like it will tear itself out of me.

The drive from El Dorado Hills to Paradise, Washington is somewhere between twelve and thirteen hours. We made good time by driving in shifts and peeing in the RV's bathroom. We reached Rainier National Park around eight in the morning, local time. I was last to drive, and I parked us in the common lot. The four of us split the cost of parking, as if we fully intended on camping where we were allowed. As soon as I got out of the RV, I noticed a difference in the air. It was so much cleaner than city air, but somehow also more textured. As well as its damp, earthy quality, I detected the sweet, strong smell of the evergreen, and the smokiness of nearby campfires. I already felt much better.

From the lot we hiked up to Moon Mountain and wandered from the trail when we were sure no one was around to notice. Only the trees watched. They stood all around us like many limbed sentries, decked in myriad shades of green, and capable of only swaying. Tony said he knew where he was going. We all just went along with it. In a clearing on the side of the mountain, we set up camp. Tony and Hank got a fire going. I gathered stumps and stones for us to sit on. Bryan grilled up some meat patties he'd formed and seasoned back home. We ate them on sesame buns with spicy mustard and American cheese. Afterwards, we sat around the fire. Tony broke out the whiskey. We sat, silent.

Tony opened his backpack and dug out several items I, at first, couldn't identify. As he began to snap the pieces together, I realized what they were. What the pieces made up.

"You brought your gun?" Hank said, beating me to the punch.

Tony grinned. "Didn't you, white boy?"

"Nah, I had to sell mine a while back."

Without getting up, Tony dragged the bag over to Hank. "Lucky for you, I brought an extra." Hank immediately started rooting through the bag for the other disassembled rifle. Tony nodded toward Bryan and me. "What about you two?"

"I brought this," Bryan said, patting the machete sheathed on the side of his bag.

"I didn't bring anything larger than a buck knife," I said. I neglected to mention that for the last three years I'd written numerous letters advocating for stricter gun laws and campaigned against animal cruelty.

Tony nodded and kept putting the gun together. When he finished, he racked it and turned to look me at me, eyes blazing but features otherwise unmoving.

"Seen you looking at my wife back there," he said.

I sniffed. My eyes shifted. My brain fumbled for something to say.

"No need denying it. No need to be ashamed either. She's a fine piece of woman."

"Yeah," I croaked.

"You want her?"

"What?"

"You heard me."

"Well, I . . ."

I felt myself shrink inside. This was gonna get bad. I held his gaze though. Even with that gun in Tony's hands, I didn't want to show him, or the others, any signs of weakness. I licked my lips, but had no spit. I blinked. He started laughing. The others joined him, albeit shakily. I tried to grin but imagined I was grimacing. The laughter died down.

"Just fucking with you, man. What happened with you and yours anyhow?"

I shrugged. "Didn't work out, I guess."

Hank finished his shot and poured himself another.

"Come on, man. Gotta be more to the story than that. She fuck around on you?" Tony asked.

"I don't know."

Tony raised his eyebrows. "You fuck around on her?"

"No! No, we just grew apart. That's all."

Tony eyed me another few seconds. It felt like a full minute. Finally, he nodded. "That's some shit."

I drank the rest of my shot and relished its burn. Then I poured another.

"Yeah," I said. "Yeah, that's some shit."

We all went silent again for a while. Hank broke it by saying he was glad we finally got to do this. We finished our whiskey and retired to our tents to nap for a little. No one had really done much sleeping during the drive. An hour or two of shuteye would do us some good. I didn't sleep though. I lay awake with a large rock pressing into my lower back. I thought about Tony asking me if I wanted to fuck his wife. Tony with his immovable gaze. Tony with his rifle. I thought I'd hear that weapon cocking the rest of my life.

I'd been friends with him the longest. He'd been on the football team, but once that season ended, he ran indoor and outdoor track. Had we gone to different schools, we'd have been fierce rivals. Since we were on the same team, our competition stayed friendly. We were constantly trying to outdo each other. Sometimes my time would be better. Other times, he'd outpace me. In tenth grade, he invited me to a party with his football teammates. The cops had shown up, and the two of us escaped together, running like mad through an open field and ducking into a patch of woods trying to hold in our laughter as flashlight beams scanned the area. After that, we were inseparable, until he left community college for business school. We'd stayed in contact though, mostly through social media, where we watched each other settle into careers and suburban domesticity.

I wondered if he would've shot me earlier had I answered his question about Yvette in the affirmative.

Nah, I thought. *Not Tony. He isn't a killer. None of us are.*

Even as I thought this, I reminded myself you can never really know anyone. A fact that had become all too clear during the dissolution of my marriage.

•••

Not long after Wiley's birth it dawned on me that though Ayla loved me, she didn't like me. I saw it in her eyes whenever we had people over, and I'd go off about politics or religion. Usually these rants came out after four or five drinks. When she and I met, we enjoyed debating these topics. She identified as Christian; I was spiritual, not religious. She considered herself a moderate Republican; I never voted. We came together on a few key things: first, we enjoyed these arguments; second, we had great sex; and third, we each thought the way we did because we cared about people.

As our relationship went on, she began to feel at odds with her party and we both started voting Democrat. Her, because she'd evolved on several key issues like gay marriage, healthcare, and the environment. Me, because if our country did implode, I wanted to be able to say, "Hey, I tried." Even though we came together on that, we drifted further apart on religion. I went full atheist while she became an active member of her church, which seemed to contradict her liberalizing, but that's Californian Christianity for you.

Our goals also held us together those first few years. I pursued my doctorate in American History and worked on *The Hangman's Gambit* whenever I could. After she graduated, she opened her interior design business. We lived in a small apartment. Seeing each other sometimes proved difficult. Despite those drawbacks, we were each working toward things. We had our separate goals and our mutual goal of getting a house in the suburbs and having some kids. Sounds basic, I know, but short of going off to live in the woods like Thoreau, it was the only way we knew how to simplify without living somewhere small and unsafe. It was nice feeling like there was something ahead for both of us, individually and collectively.

During the last year of my doctorate, I got a book deal for *The Hangman's Gambit*. A medium-sized New York press paid a five-figure advance to publish the manuscript in trade and digital. I'd been told that shit never happened anymore. Guess I was told wrong. I got a job at California State. We bought a house, not in El Dorado Hills, but in a decent neighborhood just the same. Ayla's business grew so much she hired on an assistant. Wiley came along about a year after we got settled in.

We did everything right and then some. The goddamn American Dream wasn't dead and we were living proof. I should've known it was too fucking good to be true.

The Hangman's Gambit did not sell as well as expected. The run started out okay, but then some book blogger with a chip on her shoulder decided she didn't like how I portrayed women or minorities in my novel. And that was all it took to sink the book. I was a racist, misogynist prick, and probably also a secret Nazi. Never mind my straight white male characters were also dirtbags. Never mind my best friend was black. Never mind I voted Democrat, donated to Planned Parenthood, and came out every year for the Women's March. Though my book wasn't outright banned or pulled, sales tanked so badly a second book contract was impossible.

I got depressed. Part of it might have been post-partum depression, which, it turned out, also affected dads. The book's failure was a huge factor, too, though. After all, I'd dreamed of being a professional writer since I was seven years old. I'd been denied, maybe forever. Other factors were in play, too, of course. During her pregnancy, Ayla had stopped drinking and maintained her sobriety after Wiley's birth. I did not, and after the book failed, I started drinking a lot more. Add to that the fact that giving birth had completely annihilated Ayla's sex drive and you had a perfect storm of frustrated, drunken misery.

I wanted something. Not just sex or money or success as a writer. I wanted that unattainable *something* I believed we all wanted, something that couldn't even be put into words. You could call it spiritual, but that word's been so cheapened over time, I felt dirty using it. My nighttime drives through dark, winding roads made that something feel close. So did getting so drunk I loosened my tongue and vented all my frustration to Ayla, who simply told me to try seducing her or getting a second job or writing another book. Most of all, she said I should slow down on my drinking.

"We have a kid now," was her mantra.

Maybe she'd been right about all those things. Still, she never made it seem like she *wanted* to be seduced. A second job would keep me from being a more present father. Writing another book was impossible; that book blogger had forever tarnished my name. I told Ayla all this, but she never listened. It always came back to my drinking. She could do no wrong. I felt more alone than any married man should feel.

I never cheated though. Don't get me wrong: I came close many times. Getting propositioned by hot, young students. The times I went to bars and noticed my type of woman looking lonesome. The time Wiley's babysitter had me pick her up from a party that had gotten out of control: she'd asked me not to tell her parents and said she'd do *anything* to repay me. Through all this, I stayed faithful. Sometimes this meant I had to beat my dick in the shower.

No, I didn't cheat; she did. I should've known something was fishy. Woman never worked out a day in her life, and all of a sudden, she started caring about her figure. Weight training, cardio, kickboxing. You name it, she did it, or at least tried it. I ignored the voice in my head telling me she was doing this to attract another mate. Even when nights she left me to handle Wiley's routine became more frequent. Even when I met her trainer: a man so gorgeous, even I considered switching teams. Even when I saw the outright disdain in her eyes whenever we had company and I was on one of my rants. Granted, I was usually shit-bombed in the latter scenario, and likely being obnoxious, but I didn't think it warranted such a glare. Sometimes I thought she outright hated me.

But no, there wasn't someone else. Couldn't be. She wasn't a cheater.

But she was. I guess I didn't know her like I thought I did.

Maybe I didn't know myself either.

I can't decide which is worse.

I miss Wiley.

•••

After our naps, we shared some trail mix and went on a hike. There's nothing like mountain air. It has a crispness, a purity that air closer to sea level just doesn't have. And city air, forget it. There's no comparison. Breathing in and out as we hiked made me feel a long-forgotten vitality. I felt truly pure. *Honest.* And the view. *Goddamn.* Peaks and trees for endless miles. I considered taking some photos, but I couldn't stand to distill these sights in any way, shape, or form. This was for me and only for this moment.

I didn't share any of this with my companions. Instead, I joined them in talking about pussy. Hank talked about the occasional white trash babe he picked up at his local watering hole. Tony, unsurprisingly, talked about his encounters with his lovely wife. I kept my stories relegated to women I'd fucked before I met Ayla and embellished tales of women I'd met since the divorce. Bryan said his only experience with pussy was a sexual assault in which a woman in a miniskirt took off her panties and sat on his face while he was sleeping.

"Shit, I wish I'd get assaulted like that," Hank said.

"Yeah, me too," I muttered.

"A woman would only do that to a man she knew was gay," Hank said.

Tony grinned. "Sometimes Yvette will do that to me."

"When you're sleeping?" I asked.

He shrugged one shoulder. "We have an agreement."

"An agreement?"

He laughed, a rich and mischievous sound, but he didn't elaborate. Looking at him in the afternoon light, I recognized, not for the first time, why he'd managed to get so far. He had a way about him. He carried himself with a confidence seldom seen outside the world of professional sports. He had a winning smile. A body just as toned, if not more so, than it'd been in high school. He embodied tall, dark, and handsome. I recognized these were odd thoughts for a straight man to have, but I had them just the same. Dude was charming.

"Ick," Bryan said. "You guys are gonna make me vomit."

He said it in a classic gay guy lisp he didn't have back when I knew him in high school.

"Does some switch in your head that makes you talk like that get flipped when you come out of the closet?" I asked.

"Oh-ho, shit," Tony said, covering his mouth as he laughed.

Hank laughed, too, but also tried to hide it.

"You know that's offensive, right?" Bryan asked. "I mean, you can't be that dense."

Heat filled my face. "I mean, yeah, but I guess . . . I, um . . . sorry."

"Hey, we're all friends here, right?" Tony said.

"Hard to argue with the man with a gun," Bryan said. "But no, I'm not mad or anything. Just, you know, try to think before you talk. Maybe speak with the tact you show in your writing."

"So you've read my stuff?" I asked.

"Of course. I didn't think your book was offensive either. You just tried to be real."

"I appreciate that," I said. "Really."

"We're friends."

I almost dug deeper after that comment. Was that the only reason he liked the book? Or defended it? I itched to know, but at my age you learn showing such insecurity is improper, so I stayed quiet.

We hiked on. Some miles later, we circled back so we could reach camp by sundown. When we arrived, Tony and Hank restarted the fire. I helped Bryan dish out some chicken salad and pour more whiskey. Seated around the fire, we ate in relative silence. Occasion- ally, Hank burped. The fire crackled. The sky turned orange then purple then black. All four of us perked up at the sound of nearby howling.

"The hell was that?" Hank said. "Coyote?"

"Nah," Tony said. "Sounded bigger. Wolves."

"There are wolves in Washington?" Bryan asked.

"Shit yeah, there are," Tony said. "Wanna go hunting?"

At this, my guts clenched.

Hank said, "I don't know, man. I might be too drunk."

"You ain't had any more to drink than the rest of us," Tony said.

"Yeah, but . . ." Hank drifted off, then shook his head. "Tolerance ain't what it used to be."

"Whatever you say, man," Tony said.

The wolves howled again. They sounded close. I wondered how close. Had to be damn near ten of them. I was starting to rethink my position on guns. Tony must have detected something because he slapped my arm.

"Hey, man. We leave them alone, they'll leave us alone. Right?"

I nodded. "Yeah, right."

"We should tell ghost stories," Bryan said. We all looked at him. "What? It could be fun."

"You know any ghost stories?" Tony asked.

"I know a few," Hank said.

Now we all turned to Hank.

"Bet you do," Tony said. "Bet you seen some shit."

"I have."

"So, let's hear it. Spook us." Hank looked down. He seemed to be considering something. "What are you waiting for?"

"Trying to think of one that isn't so damn depressing."

At this, we all laughed. Not only had Hank seen some shit, we knew he'd been through some shit. I remembered a selfie he took the day he got out of rehab a few years back. He'd captioned it, *Drugs kicked my ass, but they can't kill me, I'm still here.* Opiates had been his drug of choice. Apparently pain pills were a hot commodity in the moving business. I wondered if he was even supposed to be drinking alcohol with us, but he hadn't said otherwise, so I figured it best not to ask.

"All right, got something." We all leaned in to listen. "My Uncle Davey was a bartender in Hollywood Hills. Got all sorts of characters coming in for drinks and chatter. The strangest though, he told me, was a man that went by the name Mr. Boggs. According to my uncle, the man was always on about religion and black magic and communing with the devil. Just weird shit you don't say in public unless there's something off about you. The hell of it was, though, this Mr. Boggs didn't seem crazy. He was well-spoken, calm and collected. He was always well-groomed and dressed in expensive suits. The only thing that wasn't quite right was the way he smelled. Uncle Davey said the man always smelled like he'd been sitting next to a fire."

"Kinda like we are now," Bryan said.

"Guess so, maybe. Maybe not. Anyway, one of these nights, this Mr. Boggs asks Uncle Davey to come with him to some kind of meeting where he and his friends were going to contact Satan. Now, Uncle Davey was a Roman Catholic, so séances and satanic rituals were off limits. Naturally, he tells Mr. Boggs 'no' but wishes him luck. Even tells the strange man he'll pray for him. To this, Boggs only smiled lightly, without showing any teeth. My uncle used the word 'ironic' to describe Boggs' smile. Without another word, Mr. Boggs leaves.

"Now, Mr. Boggs was a regular at this point. Came in something like three times a week. But after that night, he stopped coming. Every time someone came in on one of these regular nights, Uncle Davey glanced up, expecting to see the weirdo. But he never does. On Uncle Davey's off nights, he wonders if Boggs is simply avoiding him, and he starts asking the other bartenders if they've seen Boggs. All of them say 'no.'

"Something like a month goes by. Uncle Davey starts to forget about Boggs. But then one night, Boggs is already there when Uncle Davey comes in for his shift. Boggs looks up and grins at Uncle Davey. This time he shows teeth. Uncle Davey told me he still sees that grin every time he has a nightmare. I should probably mention that—to this day—Uncle Davey can't tell this story without sobbing like a little baby. I've seen him tell it plenty of times. By the end of it, he's always a blubbering mess.

"Anyway, he goes behind the bar and asks Mr. Boggs if he needs a refill. Boggs says, 'That won't be necessary, I just wanted to give you these.' And he hands my uncle a stack of photographs. Then he leaves without another word. My uncle starts looking through the photographs. The first picture shows a large hill from a distance. The details aren't so great. A second photo is again of the hill, but this time, the one taking the picture is standing closer. The hill has what my uncle calls a 'sinewy' quality. Says it almost has the quality of captured motion. But like the first photo, this one has a gray tint to it; it's not quite black and white, but it's close. Because of that, it's still hard to make out what he's looking at.

"He looks at the third photo. The hill is closer now. He's not sure, but he thinks the sinewy bulges are people all laid down on the hill. And it looks like someone's standing over all of them. Also, there's a ravine or some kind of large winding tube going from the top of the hill to the bottom, and the people lying on the hill are . . . gathered around it somehow. The fourth photo, the man at the top of the hill is in focus. He's got a face my uncle describes as . . . fuck, what was that word? Oh, yeah. 'Bestial.' Like, wild or animal-like, I think."

"That's right," I said.

Hank held my gaze, then nodded. This didn't feel like story time anymore. Something about this story gave me the creeps. I bet the others felt it, too. All of us were at the literal edges of our seats, staring wide-eyed at Hank, who'd lost all the color in his face. His features now looked drawn and wasted.

"The man beast in the photo was very short, a midget, basically. But the winding tubular thing turns out to be his . . . well, his dick." The three of us listening sat up straight. "And the people are reaching for it with their hands and . . . and their mouths.

"He flips to the next photo, and this is when Davey usually loses it when telling this story. He flips to the next photo, and the people laid across the hill are now in focus. They're his fucking family members. *My* fucking family members. He sees his wife and kids. His parents and grandparents. My parents. My other uncles and aunts. My cousins. Me. We're all either teething on this midget devil's massive cock or caressing it. Uncle Davey says all our eyes are glazed and rolled back like we're on some kind of heavy drug, or like we're, you know, coming."

Bryan laughed out loud.

Hank shot him a glare. "Hey, fuck you. This is my goddamn family."

"I'm sorry, Hank," Bryan said. "What are you saying? Your family's cursed?"

Hank shrugged. "Feels like it sometimes."

"Ah, that's bullshit, man," Tony said. "You skipped college and went straight to work. Didn't bother making yourself marketable. Can't blame that on Satan."

"Almost everyone in my family has struggled with substance abuse. Most of us die young, except Uncle Davey, weirdly enough. It's like he's the one that's got to tell us."

"I'm sorry," Bryan said again. "That's just crazy."

Tony nodded toward me. "What do you think?"

"I think anything's possible," I said. "Most likely though, Uncle Davey's probably mentally ill."

"Last time I tell you cocksuckers a ghost story," Hank said.

"Hey," Tony said, "we're just having a little fun, right? Anyone want to go next?"

Hank softened.

"I'll go," I said, and everyone turned to me.

I told them about something I stumbled upon during my research for *The Hangman's Gambit*. Like Hank's tale of the devil and his bartending uncle, mine was set in Hollywood. Unlike his story, though, mine boasted multiple sources. All of them were anonymous internet trolls, sure, but they all said pretty much the same thing. A girl named Marielle came to Hollywood with dreams of becoming a star.

She fell in love with a famous director. Many names got thrown around in identifying this man, but Stephen Ward came up the most. She suffered tremendous abuse and eventually was killed by the guy, who wrote her story as a screenplay. Supposedly anyone who tried to film this screenplay either died or went completely crazy. According to legend, the script wound up in the hands of Stephen's son William, who managed to set Marielle free, but it cost him and his girlfriend their lives. Crazy as the story was, all of these people were real. All of them had died under mysterious circumstances.

"I think I read a book about that," Bryan said. "It was called *Mania* or something."

"Whoa, really?" I said. I hadn't heard of it.

"Yeah, I forget the author's name though."

"Was the book any good?" Hank asked.

"Eh, it was okay. Kinda fell apart in the third act."

"Most books do," I said. "Endings are hard."

"You managed to end yours pretty well," Bryan said.

"Thanks."

Bryan shrugged. "Don't mention it."

"Want to hear my story about the ghost of a bank teller?" Tony said. At this, we all laughed. "Hey, I'm serious. He keeps the robbers away from his branch."

We all laughed harder. Tony joined us. When we all died down, we looked at Bryan.

"Whatchu got?" Tony asked.

"Nothing exciting really."

"Wait, weren't you all about that paranormal shit back in

school?" Hank asked.

"I was, but conspiracy theories just stopped being fun. That whole scene got coopted by a bunch of rightwing nuts. Aliens and Bigfoot I can buy, but tell me the Holocaust was a hoax, you can fuck right off."

At this we all nodded. We drank some more and fed the fire more logs. I looked up at the sky, tried counting the stars, and gave up before I even reached ten. With my whiskey buzz going, they were all doubling and tripling anyway. Even without that, the amount of visible stars completely dwarfed what I could see back in the city. I had a thought then about how more light only blinded you. There was some fundamental truth in that, but I was too drunk to put my finger on it. Story of my life.

Not that my drinking was really a problem. If I was an alcoholic, I was a high-functioning one. And if I was functioning, what did it matter? I guess Ayla figured it mattered. Somehow she'd convinced Judge Smart it mattered, too. I was a good father. Maybe I was a bad husband, but she wasn't exactly wife of the year either.

Tony backhanded me in the chest. I flashed a glare at him.

"You good?" he asked.

"Yeah, just thinking about shit."

"Well, that never did anyone any good," Hank said.

We all laughed. We poured another round. My head was gonna hurt like hell tomorrow, and I didn't give a shit. It was good to be here. Good to be with friends. Friends, real friends, felt more and more like a rarity the older I got. People wanted to get together, but only if it somehow related to work, or if their kids were the same age as yours. This was different. I looked back up at the stars again. This time, everything was slowly spinning. I felt my lips curve into a smile. I closed my eyes. I felt damn good.

Since we didn't pay much attention to time, I didn't know what time it was when I staggered back to my tent. All I knew was the spinning sensation was increasing. I didn't think I'd throw up, but I knew I was damn close. Good thing I stopped drinking when I did. As I lay at the edge of sleep, I thought about Hank's story of the midget devil's dick and Hank's family sucking it. I wished I could write something like that. The visceral response that story's strange imagery inspired rivaled anything I'd read in years and far eclipsed anything I'd ever written. I drifted deeper into slumber and tried to forget the awful story. I even tried praying to ward it off. I know that sounds crazy: a grown-ass man, an atheist at that, afraid of a stupid story, but sometimes, especially at the brink of sleep, the unreal seems so real knowing better doesn't mean shit. I lay there, bobbing up from the black sea of the unconscious, trying to forget the monsters that swam beneath its troubled surface. The sleep that finally took me was fitful and broken.

•••

I woke up in the middle of the night. My bladder felt like a water balloon filled to full capacity. My brain felt like it was trapped inside a clenched fist. I croaked out a curse that scratched the back of my throat and propped myself on my elbows. Just outside, the fire had been reduced to glowing embers. Whoever had gone to sleep last had forgotten to douse it. If I remembered, I'd give a Smokey the Bear P.S.A. tomorrow.

I moved with tremendous care. Everything hurt. Even the persistent chirping of crickets seemed oppressive. I didn't remember drinking *that* much, but maybe I had. Or maybe I hadn't gotten enough water during the day. I stepped past the dwindling fire and reminded myself to stay hydrated. There was water in my tent. I'd take a few gulps before going back to sleep. I reached the edge of the clearing, took out my dick with one hand and wiped my eyes with the other. As I peed, I kept my eyes closed. Though I no longer had the spins, I feared they might come back. My piss sounded incredibly loud when it hit the dead leaves at my feet. When I finished, I shook dry best I could, put my dick away, and opened my eyes.

I was face to face with a goddamn wolf. Even though I knew I'd left my buck knife in the tent, I reached for my hip, where it would've been anyway. Not that a knife would be much help against this monster. It was twice the size of Tony's German shepherd, which is to say it was fucking massive. Its eyes gleamed in the starlight. Its snout was wrinkled up into a silent snarl. If it started growling, I knew for sure I'd piss again, this time soaking my pajama pants. The wolf and I stared each other down. I wanted to look away because I was pretty sure meeting its gaze would be seen as a challenge, but I was afraid to move. I was afraid to speak. Even breathing seemed ill-advised. Despite reservations, I slid one foot back. The wolf glanced down to follow the motion with a glare. Now it did growl.

"Shit," I said.

The wolf bent its legs, prepared to pounce. Its white teeth shone like ivory daggers. I forgot my hangover, even as my pulse throbbed like underwater explosions in my head. The growl of the beast grew louder, more timorous, which was worse: a scared animal is even more dangerous. I took another trembling step backwards. The wolf leaned all its weight back. It was going to jump on me any minute. Running would do me no good. By the time I turned, it'd be upon me, pinning me facedown and taking a bite out of the tense meat between my neck and shoulder.

Something exploded. The wolf yelped and dashed off to the side, scurrying away, fading into the black like a silver and gray ghost. I turned to see Tony with his rifle pointed up in the air. My mouth worked, trying to find the words to express some kind of gratitude, but I made no sound. He just nodded at me and went back to his tent. The throb of my hangover returned. So did the bone-deep exhaustion. Yeah, I'd be drinking less tomorrow. I padded back to my tent, gulped down a generous helping of water and tried to sleep.

•••

When I came out of my tent the next morning, my hangover had dulled. Everyone else was already awake. They looked at me and burst out laughing.

"You really show your dick to a wolf?" Hank said.

"I didn't know it was there."

"Divorce has made you a desperate man," Bryan said.

I gave him the finger and sat down on a stump. The fire was at full strength again. I remembered my intended spiel about putting it out before bed. I needed to wake up some more before I lectured anyone. Tony passed me a steaming mug of black coffee. I smelled it and took a sip.

"Fuck yeah, dude. Just what I needed."

"Something strong and black, huh?" he said and winked.

We all laughed about that one. Breakfast was eggs, home fries, and ham. We did some more hiking, ate salami and cheese sandwiches for lunch, talked about sex some more, gathered firewood, and spent time alone in our respective tents. I did some journaling and nodded out for a few minutes intermittently. When evening rolled around again, Tony and Hank said they wanted to go on a wolf-hunt. Since there wasn't really anything else to do, Bryan and I reluctantly agreed. We waited for total darkness and listened for the howling. It started up and we headed toward it. The more we followed it, the farther off it seemed to get. But then it fell silent for a while and we stood still. We all looked to Tony, but he stayed poker-faced, flexing his hands on his rifle's stock.

"Dude," Hank said, but Tony put up a hand to silence him.

My gaze flitted around the thick, dark woods. A sinking feeling overcame me. This was a terrible fucking idea. What the hell were we doing? As far as I knew, none of us were professional hunters. I sure as shit wasn't. If my three buddies' Facebook pages were anything to go off of, neither were they. I opened my mouth to suggest going back, but closed it again when the howling resumed. From the sound of it, the wolves were all around us and very close by.

"We should split up," Tony said.

"Are you nuts?" Bryan asked.

"Hear me out: Hank and I each got a gun. I'll make sure you two are covered."

"Why are we even doing this?" The words spilled out of my mouth before I could put them back inside. I expected everyone to ridicule me, except maybe Bryan, but only Tony spoke up.

"Hey, man, what happened to you? You used to be all about a little adventure."

"I could be asking you the same thing," I said. "Adventure's one thing, but this . . . hunting animals illegally . . . dangerous animals at that . . . this is just nuts."

More howling filled the air. The mournful, bestial chorus silenced me. We all glanced around frantically. All of us but Tony. I thought my wondering was more than valid. Something must have happened to him, too, for him to want to test himself like this. I couldn't imagine what it might be. The man had everything, yet here he was chasing one of nature's most vicious creatures, a whole pack of them by the sound of it. I tried to imagine being somewhere else, and it almost worked. It almost worked, but then I remembered why I'd come up here in the first place. I needed to get away from the day-to-day, from me, from the weak worm of a man who'd let his ex-wife take his little boy away. As if by fucking her personal trainer she hadn't emasculated me enough. Fucking bitch. That was why I was here. I couldn't speak for the others, but it had to be for similar reasons. At the very least, we had in common the hope of escaping our confinement. Even Bryan, out of the closet almost a decade now, had to be caged somehow by something. Every man living in society was, if you believed Thoreau. Maybe Tony saw the thrill of the hunt as a way of freeing himself from modern life's shackles. As our leader—and whether we'd elected him or not, I think we had an understanding he was our leader—maybe I needed to trust him. Maybe we all needed to, especially now if the wolves were onto us. As if to remind me, they howled again.

"All right," I said. "I'll go with Tony."

The corner of his mouth twitched upwards. He nodded at me. "My man."

I followed him into the dark.

•••

The cacophonous chirping of crickets started up again. I couldn't decide if it was better or worse that I was sober. I assumed the latter. Tension held every last one of my muscles. Even deep breaths of the clean air didn't soothe my anxiety. The darkness around us was complete.

"Haven't heard a wolf in a while," I said in hopes of persuading Tony to head back to camp. I hated the tremor in my voice. Hoped he wouldn't notice it.

"Maybe they're scared of something."

"Like what?" As far as I knew, they had no natural predator. Maybe he was alluding to my own fear. Letting me know he heard it.

"Like us."

"Yeah, right."

"No, really. They aren't stupid. They know what this gun can do."

I couldn't help but laugh at that. He turned to me, frowning.

"You know how crazy you sound, right?" I said with a nervous giggle.

"Something about the wilderness brings it out in a man, don't you think?"

"Funny, I was thinking about that earlier." My voice had leveled out.

"Yeah?"

"Yeah. I mean, well, sort of. About the animal in man and whether or not it's a good thing that life's demands keep it . . ."

"On a leash?"

"Exactly."

"What do you think?"

"I don't know. I mean, in class I've made the argument it wasn't such a good thing. That society and so-called civilized life keeps our true selves contained. That it's contrary to actual freedom, and maybe that's true, but I don't know. A pussy like me probably wouldn't last long in the wilderness."

"You'd be surprised, man."

"How do you figure?"

Leaves rustled. Not too close, but not too far, either. Tony kept facing forward, gun pointed into the black ahead. His expression reminded me of the time I'd seen him fight. One of his teammates got too handsy with a girl at a party. Tony stepped in. His buddy shoved him and something switched in Tony's eyes. They went cold, almost lifeless. He knocked the other guy out with one punch. Seeing that same iciness did nothing to ease my tension.

"A friend of mine used to train fighters," Tony said, pulling me out of the memory. "Said one of his toughest students was a little white boy. Hundred ten pounds soaking wet. Total animal in the ring."

"Huh. Crazy."

My voice sounded small, almost childlike. Dwarfed by the

darkness around us. Somehow Tony seemed larger than life. I remembered all the times we'd raced. Sometimes he beat me; other times I beat him. The only constants were our friendship and that, each time, the victor didn't win by much. Often, victory only became clear in the race's final seconds. I didn't feel that way now. I felt, instead, I'd come to an imaginary finish line a long time ago, but Tony had kept on running, gaining more and more ground, somehow growing stronger with every stride. Reward after reward awaited him at various intervals. I wasn't jealous. He'd busted his ass. Instead I wondered where the fuck I went wrong.

More movement in the leaves ahead. A twig snapped. It was a hollow, but resonant sound. These sounds were much closer than before.

"Can you see anything?" I whispered.

Tony shook his head. I shone my flashlight toward the noise. The illumination only made the foliage a lighter gray than before. My bladder felt full again, but I didn't want to stop because that would only drag this out longer, and God, I wanted so badly to go back to the tent and maybe to go home altogether, but I wasn't sure if I had a home anymore because Ayla had taken Wiley away and I was sick of my job and I doubted I could write another book and I just wanted to get laid, so for a moment, however brief, I could feel alive again, but the rest of the time I wanted to be too drunk to feel.

I shook my head of the rambling thoughts. I, or whoever was speaking in my head, sounded like an angst-riddled teenager. No wonder my life was in such a sorry state.

"You good?" Tony said. "You're shaking that flashlight."

I looked down at my hand which was, indeed, trembling. I willed it to stop.

Wiley. Wiley, please, whatever your bitch mother says, don't forget me. Don't forget I love you. Don't forget I was a good father, even if I came up short as a husband. Please.

More movement up ahead. Closer.

I couldn't take this. I wanted to turn and run. My bladder felt stretched to capacity. I thought if I moved at all I'd piss. Fuck, I'd never hear the end of that.

Another howl tore through the night. It sounded harsher than all the ones preceding it. I inferred all sorts of feelings in its tone. Pain. Rage. Grief. Most frightening of all, I thought it held a human quality, which had to be my imagination. Following the sound, whatever had moved in the foliage ahead moved again, this time much faster. It was headed toward that awful howl. I turned the flashlight toward the scrambling. The beam fell on a clearing and a pale shape staggered into its light and froze.

The woman was filthy. Dressed in rags. Legs unshaven. Hair in knots. Face caked with mud. Emaciated to the point I could see the impressions of her ribs. She faced us. Her wide eyes shone silver in the light. We stared at her. She stared at us. Tony lowered his rifle. I kept the flashlight on her, but my hand was shaking again. A small wet spot had formed on the front of my jeans. Turned out I did pee a little. Damn it.

The three of us stood in silence, watching each other, waiting to see who made the first move and what that move would be. From somewhere far away, Hank screamed.

The woman ran toward the scream and we followed. I couldn't tell you what Tony was thinking. I didn't even know what I was thinking. We just ran after her. Pushing through low-hanging branches. Jumping over roots and stones. It was like we were racing again. Only I wasn't in as good of shape as I used to be. The mountain air, once so clean and refreshing, now felt harsh and cold as it tore its way down my throat, in and out of my lungs. Sweat poured into my eyes, blurring my vision. Through this, I thought I saw some sort of weapon in the woman's hand. A hatchet, maybe. No, I thought, couldn't be.

Hank screamed again, and Bryan screamed, too. A loud report from the other rifle shredded the air. And then Bryan was calling our names. Calling for help.

"You hear that shit?" Tony said.

"Yes," I huffed.

"Hey, we're coming!" Tony hollered.

"Hurry!" Bryan again.

Up ahead, the woman pushed on. She seemed tireless. I didn't know how much longer I could go on. Even Tony was huffing and puffing now. Wounds glistened on his toned arms from where branches had scratched him. The left side of my abdomen started to burn. It felt like someone had stabbed me there with a hot knife. I wasn't sure what I'd do first: throw up or pass out. I was going to do one or the other, maybe both, if we didn't stop running soon.

Hank stopped screaming. Bryan wailed. Dread turned my legs to stone. Panic fluttered in my guts like a butterfly on meth. I wanted to turn and run the other way. I didn't want to see whatever awaited us up ahead. But Tony kept running, so I kept running, too.

The woman dived through a thick patch of foliage. We followed. Tony grunted and I yelped as we pushed through stabbing, scratching twigs. I prayed none of the leaves were poison ivy. Finally, we fell through the final stretch of bramble and into a clearing. What I saw brought no relief.

Hank was lying on the stony path. He had a chunk torn out of his shoulder. Bryan had removed his shirt and was pressing it to the wound. The white shirt was already soaked. It had turned completely crimson. Hank's face was very pale. His eyes streamed, tears running into his beard. When Bryan saw the woman, he blinked several times, as if he couldn't believe his eyes. I supposed he couldn't. All of this had become beyond belief.

"Where?" the woman said.

"What?!"

Bryan spoke shrilly. Confused. Hysterical. Like we all were.

"Where did he go?" she said.

"Who?"

"The one who did this."

"It wasn't any *he*," Bryan said. "It was some kind of . . ."

"Wolf," she said. "I know. I have to go after him."

"Now, wait a minute," Tony said. "The only thing we need to do is get my friend some help. We're in the middle of nowhere and he's bleeding to death."

"It might be best if he did," she said.

"What?!" I think we all screamed that.

"Never mind." She looked at Bryan. "Which way did he go?"

Bryan pointed a shaky finger into the surrounding darkness. The woman moved to run in that direction, but Tony caught her by the elbow.

"Wait a damn minute. First, I think you owe us an explanation."

She jerked her arm away.

"How do you figure I owe you anything?"

"I figure whatever you're after took a chunk out of my friend's arm."

"Fuck you." She spat in his face and marched toward the place Bryan had pointed. This time I caught her. I grabbed her from behind around her waist. I tried not to think about her naked ass against my crotch. She squirmed against me. "Let me go!"

"Just hang on, okay?" I said. "We need to get my friend some medical attention and you . . . you don't look like you're in any shape to go off chasing wolves."

She started to relax in my arms. I didn't let her go. She hadn't earned my trust.

"Anyone bring their phone?" Tony asked.

"Mine's back at camp," Bryan said.

"Mine, too," Hank said through gritted teeth.

Tony nodded in my direction. I shook my head.

"All right," he said. "We head back to camp. Bryan and I will help Hank." He looked at me. "Don't let this one out of your sight."

"You can let me go. I'm not gonna run," the woman said. "He's probably too far off for me to catch up to him by now."

"Why do you keep saying 'he'?" Tony asked. "It's a wolf, right?

Just an animal."

Her jaw tightened. She looked down.

"He's my son," she said.

Tony and I exchanged glances. I loosened my hold on her but didn't release her completely. I was testing her. Had to see if she'd try to break free. Except for her labored breathing, she remained still.

"Your son is a wolf?" Tony said, shooting me another look, one that said, *This bitch is crazy.*

"It's a long story."

"Yeah, well, I'd like to hear it. I think you should come back to camp with us."

"You wouldn't believe a word I say."

Tony took the gun Hank was using and tossed it my way. I caught it with one hand. The woman didn't try to escape.

"All the same," Tony said. "You look like you could use some food. Some sleep. Maybe a bath."

The mention of her unwashed state made me aware of her smell. It was like wet dirt mixed with blood and body odor. Still, I found myself wanting her. I couldn't explain why, and part of me felt gross about it. Another part told me it was perfectly natural. Biology. The thrill of the hunt.

She wriggled out of my one-armed grasp and stood between Tony and me. She held up her hatchet. Tony and Bryan helped Hank to his feet.

"You said you have food?" she said.

"Yes," Tony said.

"All right. I'll come back to your camp. Just don't expect me to stick around if someone comes to rescue us." Her gaze traced the gleaming curve of her hatchet. "I've still got a job to do." Now she looked back at me. "And if any of you tries to rape me, this hatchet's going in your groin."

•••

We hiked back to camp. We considered hiking back down Moon Mountain to drive Hank to the hospital, but we figured he'd need attention quicker. Maybe someone could send a helicopter up here. Airlift him. None of our phones worked.

Bryan dressed Hank's wound the best he could. Tony stood watch at the edge of camp. I found the woman some clothes: sweat pants and a tank top. She thanked me and got dressed. I brought her a tin of sardines and she ate with grotesque enthusiasm. Of course, I didn't blame her. She looked like she'd been living on nothing but nuts and berries and maybe even crickets for months. I offered her a packet of wet wipes. She took a handful of them, scrubbed her hairy armpits and reached inside her pants to scrub her crotch. She went to hand them back to me, but I shook my head and pointed to the fire pit. She threw the now black and yellow wipes into the ashen remains.

Seeing the white and gray log shards got me thinking about building another fire. I set to work while the others watched. Hank was sitting up now. Some color had returned to his face. Bryan used wet wipes to clean his hands. Tony kept his eyes toward the darkness. The rifle rested on his shoulder. More wolves howled in the surrounding forest, but none sounded as awful or unnatural as the bellow of the beast that had undoubtedly injured Hank. The wolf this strange woman said was her son.

When the fire was built, I sat down next to her. Bryan sat next to Hank. Finally, Tony abandoned his post and joined us. He laid his rifle across his lap and kept his hand near the trigger guard. When we all seemed a lot more settled, I asked the woman to tell us her long story. I can only speak for myself, but I think we all wanted some answers. Here's what she said.

Friday
9 PM to 10 PM

56 MILD, MILD WORLD OF ANIMALS
Nature. Special two-hour sloth feature.

3 **8** JOY OF FAINTING (CC)

5 **9** **12** FRIGHTLINE (CC) — Ded Koppel
News. For dead people.

10 **2** 90 MINUTES; 60 mins.
A special investigation report on false advertising.

18 THE MOLDIN' GIRLS — Comedy
Tempers are hot when the girls battle to the death for the last piece of cheesecake. Gorethy tries and fails to liven her rotten disposition.

38 TWENTY-GORE HOUR SKELETHON
Scarity event raising funds to fight osteoporosis featuring all your favorite skelebrity personalities.

22 ACACIA AVENUE (CC) — Drama
Charlotte is pursued by a strange man who attempts to put her off her career path. Things turn dark when he begins showing obsessive, possessive desires.

9:30 **24** MOVIE — Comedy; 1 hr 30 mins. ★
"My Mother Was A Teenage Dracula." (1982) A father must come clean to his teenage daughter about the true story behind her mother's death when the daughter begins exhibiting a sudden thirst for human blood.

4 **13** ENTERTAINMENT LAST NIGHT (CC)
Scheduled: Famous guitarist and his drummer argue about how loud the snare drum should have been in the final mix of their classic album.

20 TALES FROM THE DIMSIDE

RIP LOSE WEIGHT WITH DEATH — Commercial

ON MOVIE — Western; 1 hr 25 mins. ★★
"Unbridled Racism." (1964) A wealthy rancher hires a rugged gunman to protect the land he stole from being reclaimed by a pack of godless heathens.

18 RIGHTEOUS ELITE — Religion
Worldwide phenomenon pastor leads his faithful congregation.

SPECIAL ENCORE PERFORMANCE

PRIMITIVE

CHANNEL 83 WGHP

HORRORAMA

10 PM **83** MOVIE — Suspense; 2 hrs. ★★★
"Primitive." (1984) A group of friends discover a strange woman in the forest during a camping trip. She says she is looking for her son, but can she be trusted?

WOLF MOTHER

MY NAME IS LUCA BARATH and eight years ago, I gave birth to a monster. For the past year, I've been wandering this wilderness, trying to kill my child. It would take little effort for him to kill me. I suspect he'd rather not because I am, after all, his mother. To know he's still capable of such love makes what I must do infinitely more difficult. And make no mistake: for reasons that will soon become apparent I *must* do this. Chief among them is that I am his mother. He's my responsibility.

This tragedy, my tragedy, began with the miscarriages. Five of them. Five fucking babies I couldn't carry to term. You'd think after so many instances of watching your underdeveloped child flushed down the toilet, you'd be unable to feel anything. If only that were true. Every time another fetus left me as a lumpy, bloody mess of wasted potential, another place inside me tore open, left me with another scar. The worst part about it was it was all me. My husband's sperm was fine. Something was wrong with me. Some kind of uterine abnormality.

I so badly wanted a baby. Richard so badly wanted a baby. Do you know how terrible it is to know the person you love more than anything in the world wants something you feel like you're supposed to give them, but you can't give it to them? It's the most awful feeling you can imagine. The depression and feelings of inadequacy were crushing.

I turned to booze and pills to numb the pain. And they worked sometimes. Unless I stayed up too late and a powerful rage took hold. I lashed out at Richard. Told him he was putting undue pressure on me. Told him to knock up one of the neighborhood girls if that would make him happy. I always woke up in tears, of course, and feeling like a hydrogen bomb had gone off in my head. On one of these mornings, Richard told me to go to rehab and said he'd leave if I didn't. I went, but made sure he knew I was going grudgingly. Mount Sinai Rehabilitation Facility was the name of the place. It's still there, I'm sure. While I was a patient, I met a man who changed everything for me. But not in the way you'd think. His name was Cort Boggs and he smelled like fire.

•••

Something about this man staying in the same facility as me for reasons he didn't disclose made me disclose everything to him. To this day, I still don't know why. I guess, given what follows, it isn't too much of a stretch to attribute this magnetism to some kind of magic. Regardless of the reason, I told him everything, even stuff I refused to share in group. For instance, I told him why methods like adoption and a surrogate weren't options for me. That was because of my father. I came from money, but I married for love. Dad said that unless I bore him a child, I'd never see a dime of my inheritance.

I suppose I could have defied him and figured out the money later. Unfortunately, because of all my medical bills, I wasn't in any position to throw away the possibility of receiving such a significant sum of money. Richard and I were working class. Barely above the poverty line. Call me a hopeless romantic, but I thought marrying for love mattered.

My father kept on living.

The collection calls kept on coming.

My habits got more expensive.

By the time I met Cort Boggs, I was desperate. I even told him how desperate I was. I told him I would do anything to be able to have a child.

Now, I don't know if Boggs was the devil. I sure as hell didn't give him my soul. There was no contract for me to sign in blood. Nothing like that at all. Not even a verbal agreement. He simply told me what I could do and I listened. I wrote down his instructions exactly as he gave them and followed them to the letter.

I know what you're thinking: *Here's the part of the story where she says she wishes she hadn't done it.* Right? That's the hell of it though. I don't regret anything. I got what I wanted. I gave birth to a beautiful, blue-eyed baby. Not long afterwards, my father died and left me enough money to get out of debt and put a down payment on a three-bedroom dream house. For seven years, I got to be a mother to a sweet little boy.

But I'm getting ahead of myself. I should probably tell you how all this happened and how it all went horribly wrong.

•••

My child, the one I now aim to kill, was conceived in the very same wilderness surrounding us. I came here to Moon Mountain after a thirty-six hour fast. I carried only a small bundle of wolfsbane, one vial of menstrual blood, another vial containing Richard's semen, a pound of raw hamburger, a lighter, a white candle, and a lock of hair from a little boy. When I reached the mountain's peak, I dug a pit, put the meat at the bottom, drizzled the blood and semen over it, wrapped the candle in the boy's hair, arranged the wolfsbane so it made a triangle around the hole, and lit the candle. And then I waited.

The candle burned down, sizzling strands of the hair. The wind blew, but the flame stayed strong. Wolves howled, but I didn't let them scare me. If I was to die out here, at least I'd have given my life in the effort of attaining something I so desperately wanted. When the fire ran out of wax and wick, it spread across the meat, enveloping it completely. I didn't think it was supposed to do that, at least not from a physics perspective. If I wasn't convinced then I'd stepped out of the realm of known science, the flame rising as a crimson column before me made it fact. The fire took the shape of a large wolf, red-orange with black eyes. Part of me wanted to run, but I'd already come so far, and I needed whatever this demon could offer me.

Its fiery limbs enshrouded me. The heat was intense, but somehow my skin didn't burn. The wolf demon lowered me to my back.

Its member penetrated me, even though I was wearing pants. I don't know how it was possible, but again, this was beyond science.

The wolf demon and I fucked all night. I don't know how the fire kept burning or how my stamina remained so tireless. All I know is when we finished, it was morning and I was with child. I could feel a strange heat in my womb and knew it was growing and would continue to do so. There would be no miscarriages this time.

•••

Throughout the pregnancy, I had awful dreams. Giving birth to a fire that consumed me and Richard and all the nurses. Giving birth to a wolf cub that tore its way out of my stomach. Giving birth to the devil incarnate. I'm not religious. Still, the fear felt very real, very possible. I awaited my child's birth with excitement and dread. The shift between these emotions was cruel in its inconsistency. I often thought of dying.

•••

Jonathan Winstead Barath was born at 11:31 on the evening of March 16, 2010. Until I laid eyes on him, I continued to harbor fears he wouldn't be normal. Even as I pushed, sweat soaking my hairline, a feeling like tiny claws tearing me apart from the inside, over the encouraging words of Richard and my doctor, I imagined something monstrous ripping its way out of my vagina, shredding my walls, splitting me end to end, feeding on me as I bled to death and Richard watched in horror, the doctor and nurses powerless to do anything. Should such an awful scenario have occurred, it would've destroyed Richard. I didn't want that. I feared what it would do to him more than what would happen to me. I was the one who dabbled in weird wolf magic. Richard was blameless.

The slick, crying baby the doctor pulled from me was no monster. Or at least he wasn't yet a monster. Or, if he was, the bestial urges lay dormant and deep. No, on that day, he was a perfectly normal, healthy, painfully beautiful baby boy. I experienced true love at first sight.

I see the way you're all looking at me. *How can she sit here telling this story without bursting into tears?* The truth is not that I've no tears left, as you may suspect. No, it's that no amount of tears or any sort of outward display of grief can properly express what I feel. Instead, a storm of grief churns inside me. It will not dissipate until I die and I cannot die until he does.

•••

The years passed and I won't tell you everything was picture perfect. We struggled as a family, with raising a child. I know now all those struggles were normal. Back then, I didn't feel so sure. Every toddler meltdown, every act of defiance, every type of antiauthoritarian behavior all kids exhibit, I worried that *now,* now I'd see the transformation into the monster I feared he'd always become. But then, not an hour later, he'd be docile. He'd tell us he loved us. He'd play nicely with others. Want to be with us. Miss us. All normal things. All wonderful things.

I've called this story a tragedy. In every tragedy, the central character has a flaw, something that makes their whole world fall apart. Supposing this is a tragedy, my flaw was only my total love for Jonathan. My love blinded me when I should've seen the danger right away. Not a week or two after his seventh birthday, the first neighborhood kid was killed. Torn to pieces. The morning after it happened, I knew something was wrong with Jonathan, though I wasn't sure what. He looked and acted tired, like he hadn't slept at all. Moved slowly. Yawned a lot. Sported black bags under his eyes. Another peculiar thing was that his pajamas lay discarded in the corner of his room. He lay in bed naked.

After the dead child was discovered, a creeping suspicion made me draw connections, but my love smothered them into silence. Jonathan didn't change every full moon. If that had been the case, I likely would've stayed ignorant unless he made some sort of mistake that led the police to him. Maybe even then. No, it happened a lot more frequently. It happened whenever the dormant beast got hungry.

I finally allowed for the possibility Jonathan might be responsible for these murders after three children died. On each of those following mornings, he exhibited the same exhaustion, a look of dishevelment, and had taken off his clothes. He lost interest in food, except for meat, which he always asked for undercooked.

I started checking on him nightly at two-hour intervals. I hardly slept myself. Richard said I was crazy. He, of course, didn't know *why* I was doing these checks. I told him I was afraid Jonathan would wander out and get murdered himself or the killer would break in. He asked me over and over if I was using again. He didn't know the truth. He still doesn't. As far as Richard knows, his wife and son are long dead. Maybe he isn't so far off.

•••

One night in July, my worst fear finally came true. When I went to check on Jonathan a little after two o'clock, he wasn't in his bed. The scream tore itself from my lungs before I even knew it was coming. Richard rushed in. Asked what was wrong. Gasped when he saw the empty bed.

"Where is he?" he asked.

"Stay here," I said. "I'm gonna go out looking."

"We should go together," he said.

"No. Someone has to be here if he comes back."

He agreed and sat down on Jonathan's bed, looking down at his hands and probably feeling useless. In truth, I felt like he was. I loved him—I still do—but this has always been my fight.

I drove frantically through the neighborhood, my head on a swivel, nearly crashing several times into parked cars. I even almost ran over a scurrying raccoon. The fact no one called the police on me is astounding. A speeding vehicle, circling the neighborhood and swerving. It was too dark for anyone to recognize the car as their neighbor's. Probably seemed like I was casing the place, or lost and very drunk.

Damn near two hours passed. During the second hour, Richard started blowing up my phone like a jealous ex-boyfriend. I ended up switching it off. At no point did it occur to me Jonathan had come home. He couldn't have.

I parked at the edge of a patch of woods and got out. I switched my phone back on to use the flashlight, but kept it silenced. The overgrown path wove through trees impossibly tall, impossibly dense. A rich stench of foliage choked the cold air. I hugged my arms to my chest. A heavy dragging sound from the surrounding woods drew my attention. I shone my light in its direction and immediately wished I hadn't.

A nightmare version of my son, something between wolf and boy, with an upturned snout, a shaggy brown beard and mane, and pointed ears, was squatting over another boy. The victim's throat was torn open. The Adam's apple gleamed white at the center of a red, ragged hole. Blood from the wound dripped from Jonathan's beard and lips as he cradled the boy's head. He lifted his gaze to me and his pale blue eyes softened. The sight of his mother filled him with tremendous regret and shame. At least, that's how I interpreted it. Maybe it was only what I hoped.

He dropped the boy's head and it landed with a wet thud. The dead face turned toward me upon impact. Its vacant eyes stared without sight. A lump lodged itself in my throat. I could do nothing but stare.

Jonathan stood, at least a head taller than the boy I knew. Patches of fur covered his lean physique. He looked much older than seven, but I recognized him just the same. He kept his eyes on me. I expected him to attack. Wanted him to. Instead, he ran away. I found my voice and called his name, but it was far too late. He was gone. I was alone. I called the police.

•••

I, of course, said nothing about wolf boys or sexual liaisons with demons. I simply reported the body and said my son was missing. The police asked what felt like a million questions. Neither Richard nor I got any sleep that night. The morning light brought me no comfort. Instead, it made my nightmare seem far more real. During the night, I still harbored hope it was all no more than a bad dream. In the daylight, I could deny nothing.

A month of terrible depression followed. I often thought of using again. I came pretty close a few times, but ultimately, I decided to stay sober. My son deserved a mother who would let herself feel the full brunt of her grief. Two more children were killed. I knew Jonathan was responsible, but I kept silent. At some point, he'd come home. I hoped for and dreaded this.

Jonathan came back to me one afternoon I happened to have off from work. He didn't come to the door. I'm not even sure how he got in. He walked in on me in the kitchen while I was drinking coffee that had gone cold. I didn't spit the sip I'd just taken out in surprise like people do in the movies. I simply held it in my mouth as I gazed at the prodigal son.

"Hello, Mother," he said. I couldn't find the words to respond. "I know what you saw and I know what you know. I also know what you did to make me."

I swallowed, opened my mouth, but still couldn't speak. Emotions and questions overwhelmed me. I felt tremendous relief and heartbreak. I wondered where he'd been when not killing other children. How he was able to speak like someone much older. How he knew the ugly secret of his conception. I could voice none of these things. I could only stare at him through eyes blurred by tears.

He told me he'd been to the mountains. He said he knew what he did was wrong and tried to live alone, feeding on deer and game instead. Eventually, the loneliness became too much, and he returned. I found my voice and asked how I could help him. Vowed I would do anything to ease his pain.

"I want a family," he said, and I got the awful notion he meant to rape me.

Instead he told me to call on the wolf demon again, using Boggs' spell.

"I merely want a companion. A sibling or lover, someone with whom I can share my life. When you've given me that, I'll go away, and I'll never harm another child."

"I don't want you to go away," I said.

"But I must, Mother. You know as well as I that I do not belong here."

"Yes, you do. We're family. We'll make it work."

"No," he said, shaking his head. "I've told you what must be done. If you are not with child by this time next month, I will kill again, and I will keep killing until you give me what I've asked for."

"Why can't you find someone else?" I asked, already knowing the answer.

"You're my mother. I'm your responsibility. Do this one final thing for me."

I held out my arms, needing to feel him so badly it nearly burned. His features softened and I thought, hoped, he meant to embrace me. Instead, he turned away and left me with a terrible emptiness.

•••

I went back to Moon Mountain. I took my candle, menstrual blood, raw meat, semen, hair, and wolfsbane. I completed the ritual exactly as I had before. I mention this because it seems only by some cruel chance or the malevolent will of the forces I'd conjured that things did not go as they previously had. This time, it was much worse.

After another all-night fuck marathon with the wolf demon, I staggered down the mountain as the rising sun filled the sky with something like fire. The sharp pains in my stomach came before I even made it out of the wilderness. They were so bad, I cried out, doubled over and dropped to my knees. My belly swelled up, lifting my shirt, the skin stretching taut before my eyes. The pain was exquisite and I kept crying, but no one came to my aid. I don't think anyone was even around to hear. I felt like my insides were about to explode.

Most of the pressure forced itself downward. I was going to give birth.

I dropped my pants and stayed on my hands and knees. With my eyes pinched shut, I pushed. There was no epidural to numb the agony this time. I screamed as my uterus shredded, as my cunt spread, as blood and amniotic muck spattered the dirt, as one-by-one fucking *puppies* dropped out of me. Goddamn six of them. I collapsed when I was finished. Their cries were a cacophony of pitiful suffering. I turned and saw them: horrid half-lupine babies twitching and wailing in a black, lumpy puddle.

I don't know what came over me then. I just knew these monstrosities, these abominations, could not be allowed to live. Using what little strength I had, I found the nearest large rock. One after the other, I smashed my offspring, grunting with exertion, nearly vomiting at the crunching of tiny bones and the spray of more blood. When it was finished, I collapsed again. This time, I lay among the mangled and mashed remains of my children and bellowed.

HUNT

"AND THAT WAS WHEN HE came out of the woods," Luca said. "My son watched me smash the life out of his siblings. He stood over me and said anything that happens from now on would be my fault. The blood of children, not just the brutally aborted half-wolf infants, would be on my hands.

"Since recovering, I've managed to keep him mostly to these woods, though sometimes he gets past me. I admit I've had opportunities to kill him, but something has always held me back. But I'm tired. It's time to end it forever. He must die."

She held up the hatchet, but her grip was loose. We all watched her, waiting for her to say more. All of us, that is, except for Hank. He was slumped over, exhausted. He didn't even perk up when she mentioned the name 'Cort Boggs.' I thought for sure that'd get him going, but he remained sedate. Bryan kept suggesting Hank go to sleep, but Hank shook his head and shoved Bryan away every time.

Luca said no more. She threw the hatchet between her feet and it stuck in the dirt. I considered, not for the first time, putting my arm around her. Holding her close and telling her it would be all right. After all, wasn't that what I was supposed to do? None of the other men showed any interest in consoling her. She didn't seem as though she wanted to be consoled. Her closed off posture and downcast eyes told the story of her isolation. How she didn't just expect this isolation to continue, but that she wanted it to continue. As she'd said, this was her fight.

It was a hard urge to ignore though. Seemed the most natural thing in the world. Only, maybe it wasn't. Maybe this need to console each other, in particular, men's desire to console women, was some social construct. Solitude was natural. Solitude and survival. The only exception was when survival depended on cooperation. Sometimes I felt like I was full of shit. This time was no exception.

When Luca said nothing else, Tony got up, shouldered his rifle and walked back to the edge of camp. The howling had been sporadic while we listened to Luca's tale and now it was almost nonexistent.

I turned to look at her. I examined her for any sign she wanted to let me in. Anything that said she didn't want to be alone. She gave no indication. She stared into the fire, probably thinking of monsters, but she could have been thinking of anything. Her walls were up. No one could bring them down or see through them, not even me. I thought about Ayla, about Wiley, about what the rest of my life would be like. I imagined seeing my kid on weekends, taking sexy students home on weeknights. At least for the first few years. Who knew what would happen later? After I got old and unattractive. After my kid grew to resent me as all kids grew to resent their parents. Shit, I didn't even know if I'd make it down from this fucking mountain.

Now, that was an odd thought. I wondered what brought it on. Luca's story, of course. It was ludicrous. Wolf demons, werewolf children. How gullible did she think we were? The only certainty as it related to Luca's story was she believed it. Maybe *she* was dangerous. Maybe she'd kill us all in our sleep. I looked at Tony. I had a feeling he wouldn't be sleeping at all. Maybe none of us would. Except maybe Hank.

Thinking of my old friend, now resting his head on Bryan's shoulder, made me extra shifty. We had to get him to a hospital first thing in the morning. We didn't even have to say it. I'm sure we all knew. God knew what kind of diseases that wolf carried. Or wolf boy. I shook my head and rolled my eyes. It drew Luca's attention.

"I wouldn't expect you to believe me," she said. "Any of you."

"Why would you say that?" I asked.

"It's a completely crazy story," she said.

"You can say that again," Bryan said.

"I swear it's true. Why else would I be out here?"

"I could think of a list of reasons."

"Ease off, Bryan," I said.

"What? We were all thinking it."

"I'm sure you were," she said. She turned her attention to the sleeping Hank. "You're gonna want to watch him closely."

"We'll get him to a hospital at dawn," Tony said over his

shoulder.

"I don't think a hospital will do any good. If my son's a were-wolf—"

"Look." Tony turned. "We've heard enough. He was bit by a wolf. That's all. And the wolf wasn't your son."

"It didn't look like a regular wolf," Bryan said, now inching away from Hank.

"Because it wasn't. I'm sorry I didn't make it to you in time."

Bryan, Luca, and I turned our attention back to the fire. Tony gazed into the dark woods. The howling persisted. It made me think of the old sound effects mixtapes I used to play on Halloween for Wiley. Even if Luca's story didn't contain a nugget of truth, it still affected me deeply. I feared who Wiley would grow up to be now that I wouldn't be in his life as much as before. I cursed Ayla for taking him away from me. My thoughts drifted to a dark place; I imagined strangling her in her sleep. Usually, when such thoughts surfaced, I shook them away and made myself focus on something else. Now, with the flames dancing before me, I dwelled on the awful image and the even more awful satisfaction it brought me.

Of course, killing her wouldn't help me get my son back. It would make things a lot worse. I'd get life in prison, maybe even the death penalty. Wiley would hate me forever. And would it even really be that satisfying? I suppose I would never know unless I tried, but that was one hell of a leap, one I couldn't envision myself taking. The idea of killing someone, even someone who had hurt me so pro-foundly, nauseated me. This was someone I'd loved, for fuck's sake! I now cursed myself for even entertaining the fantasy as long as I did.

Hank was lying on a log now. His eyes were closed. Drool leaked from the corner of his mouth. I thought he looked very peaceful. It didn't stop me from worrying though.

There better not be any delay in the morning. We need to get him medical attention.

In the back of my mind I heard Luca saying no hospital could help him. I hoped she wouldn't try to kill him in his sleep. He stirred, moaned, and licked his lips. Luca stared at him. I could only imagine what she was thinking. One hand dangled from her knee. It wouldn't take much for her to swipe the hatchet and bury it in his brain. I bet she was thinking the same thing. Her hand probably burned with need to hold the hatchet. The weapon had likely been the only thing to make her feel safe in the last year. While a year may not seem like a long time in our busy, hustle-and-bustle, civilized world, it probably passes like an eon out here, alone in the wilderness, on the hunt for your own flesh and blood.

Well, assuming everything she's said is true.

Not a second after I finished the thought, Hank pressed himself back up. He opened his eyes, revealing the blue eyes of a wolf. He opened his mouth, revealing massive, curved canines. Before anyone had a chance to scream, he bit into Bryan's throat and tore out a considerable fleshy chunk. Arterial spray followed, soaking Hank's face, painting it crimson. Bryan's eyes went dead and he fell over, twitching.

Luca swiped for her hatchet, pulled it from the sand, and swung the weapon. Hank ducked the blow and scrambled for the surrounding woods. Tony spun, rifle aimed, but his face slack with disbelief. His eyes were wide. His jaw worked, but he didn't speak. Hank turned to him, teeth bared and claws—fucking claws—raised, and half-howled, half-growled. Then, he raced into the devouring darkness of the woods. I rushed to Bryan's side and cradled his head, even though it was much too late to help him. I sobbed uncontrollably and watched my falling tears mix with blood.

•••

I haven't been completely honest with you. Maybe I should remedy that. Earlier in this manuscript, I made a passing reference to a homosexual experience I had when I was younger. I also said that after college, I found out Bryan was gay. While yes, he didn't come out of the closet to everyone until after college, I knew about his sexuality long before.

Throughout high school, I guess you could say I was curious. I definitely liked girls. All the porn I watched appealed to my male gaze. Sometimes, though, I wondered about guys. Bryan and I had been friends since elementary. Our parents had been friends and encouraged us playing together. I guess because I'd known him for so long, I had my suspicions about his sexuality. Sometimes I wondered what it'd be like to kiss him. Of course, I never made a move because, holy shit, what if I was wrong, and he was as straight as Tony or Hank? I let all my reservations go during that party with the drama club my senior year.

If I'd told you this part of the story before I held my dead friend in my lap, I probably would've prefaced the tale by saying I consumed a fuck ton of alcohol that night. Now, I wasn't sober, by any means, but to suggest I didn't know what I was doing wouldn't be fair to my friend's memory. So, yeah, I was buzzed, but not drunk. Even the buzz I had going was only so I could build the courage to broach the subject.

We ended up on the back patio, just he and I, reminiscing about the last few years and speculating on the future. He said he wouldn't be pursuing acting in college. Tech was where the money was and he wanted to support himself. Maybe he'd join an amateur theater troupe one day, after he'd put down some roots. I wonder if he ever did. Talk of roots led to talk about marriage. I wasn't seeing anyone, but I got with the occasional girl at Tony's football parties. Bryan said he didn't see himself getting married.

With my tongue loosened by booze, I decided to ask.

"Well, you're gay, right?" I said.

"What? No."

"Come on, man. You can tell me. We've been friends forever."

"Please, you mostly just hang out with your jock buddies anymore."

"Ah, but I'm here now, right, bro?"

He sighed, stared ahead into the dark field of his backyard. "Fine. Yes. I'm gay, but I'm not out yet, so if you tell anyone . . ."

"I won't. I promise."

"Why's it matter anyway?"

Now, it was my turn to sigh. "Well, I guess, I dunno. Ever since Cora and I broke up, I've been wondering what it was like to . . . be with a guy, and I figured, you being my friend and all . . ."

"How much did you have to drink?"

"I'm not that drunk. Besides, it's been on my mind for a while."

"All right, well, we should probably do whatever we're going to do away from the house. Don't want anyone to see."

"Yeah," I said, casting a glance back at the sliding glass door. "You're probably right."

We walked across the dark field to a patch of trees.

"So, what do you want to try?" he asked, when we were obscured from view.

"I mean, I guess we could start with a kiss."

"Sure," he said.

For a couple of seconds, neither of us moved. Then he reached for me. His touch was delicate, not at all what I expected being touched by a man would be like. The back of my neck tingled under his fingers. His lips were every bit as soft as a woman's. It wasn't long before I felt myself growing hard. One of his hands drifted down there and lightly squeezed.

"Want a blowjob?" he asked.

"S-sure," I said, all of a sudden trembling.

"If you don't want to . . ."

"No, it's fine . . . just nervous is all."

"Relax," he said, going to his knees. "You'll enjoy it."

"Have you . . . before?"

"Once or twice," he said, winking at me as he undid my pants.

His hands were cool around my shaft and I tensed. When he put me in his mouth, I practically melted into the tree behind me. The hot moisture behind his lips released all the tension I felt, long before my orgasm came on. I'd gotten a few blowjobs before. Maybe I'd

PRIMITIVE - LUCAS MANGUM

just gotten dealt a bad hand, but in my experience, high school girls used too much teeth. This was not the case with Bryan. He seemed to know exactly what I wanted. It was like a warm, wet massage on my cock. Not sure how long it took me to come, but it couldn't have been long. He swallowed, too, which was something no one had done for me before either.

I dropped to my knees and embraced him. And then I cried.

I know what you're thinking: it's 2018; being gay is no big deal. Just come out of the closet already. For me, it isn't that simple. It's never been that simple. I still liked women. Do you know how hard it is to find a woman who's willing to date a man who's slept with another man? It's like finding a unicorn. Or at least that's how it's been for me. Ayla sure as shit wouldn't have been cool with it. She even said so herself once.

I was happy when Bryan came out. Part of me envied him.

Now, as I held his lifeless body in my arms, crying in front of him again—only this time he couldn't see me—I felt another void open up inside me. I felt bereft of a potential future, but most of all, I felt the need to wreak bloody, terrible vengeance.

•••

I got to my feet. Glanced around for Hank's gun. When I found it, I marched over, picked it up and racked it. Tony and I locked eyes. He nodded at me and turned to Luca.

"Where do these wolf people hang out?" he asked.

"There's two now. There was just one, but I let your goddamn friend live."

"We'll fix that," I said.

"Our best course is to follow him. You take care of him. I'll take care of my boy."

Nods all around. We left the light of the fire behind.

The woods swallowed us. Our flashlight beams shone pitifully in the black. All around us, the crickets and toads created a Phil Spector-worthy wall of sound. Intermittent howls pierced through it. I squeezed the rifle so tightly my hands went numb. Sweat soaked the pits of my shirt and made my asshole itch. Despite my discomfort, despite the unpleasant buzz of my nerves, this wasn't like before. I didn't want to go back at all. This new mission, vengeance for Bryan, peace for Hank, would prove I'm a goddamn man.

I followed Tony. Somehow he stayed cool as spring rain. He held his rifle in a relaxed grip. His features were hard though, an intense, piercing gaze in his eyes. Luca held her hatchet at the ready. Her head turned every few steps. She was on high alert. I had no idea how the rest of this night would go. I don't think any of us did. Could she do what needed to be done? Could I? I even had my doubts about Tony. This was all uncharted, even for a tough man like him, even for a long-suffering woman like her.

We came to a clearing at the bottom of a hill. Stones jutted out from dead leaves and dry pine needles like the crumbled remains of a castle. The moon and stars cast pale luminescence across the void and made everything silver, cold, lifeless. If not for the song of crickets and wolves, or the cool breeze that carried the scent of pines, this would seem like a dead place.

At the center of the clearing, Tony stopped to look around. Luca and I joined him. The first growl came from on top of the hill. The beast that vocalized it had been behind us and we hadn't even known. I wondered how long it had been there, how long death had loomed so close. We all turned toward the sound. No creature was yet visible. It was just too damn dark out.

Another growl came from somewhere beside us.

"Was that the same wolf?" Tony asked.

"I don't know," Luca said.

Another growl.

"Are we fucking surrounded?" I said, my voice a harsh whisper.

"If we are, we'll deal with it," Tony said.

Luca raised her hatchet.

Another growl, closer. This came from the first wolf, the one atop the hill. Its eyes gleamed in the beam of my flashlight. It bared its teeth.

"Oh, shit," I said.

Tony turned, snarled.

"We should stand back-to-back," Luca said. "That way nothing sneaks up on us."

"Good call," Tony said.

We did as Luca suggested. More eyes lit up in the surrounding darkness.

"This is bad," I said.

"Shut the fuck up, Walton. Don't be a pussy."

"Both of you, shut up."

The growling grew louder as the wolves came in closer. I could see them now. Silver fur that moved like sand dunes in the wind as the muscles beneath flexed. Even the crickets and toads had fallen silent now. It was as if all were watching this standoff. This confrontation between beast and man that would only end in fatality.

What was going to set things in motion? Which wolf would pounce first? Which human would fire off a shot or swing an axe? The chorus of growls added to the tension. Each growl was something bigger rumbling into life. Release had to come. But only bloodshed could bring it.

Tony fired the first shot. The slug tore a bloody chunk from the shoulder of the wolf on the hill. The wounded beast yelped. Another beast leapt. Tony turned toward it and fired. This shot proved more effective, blowing off the top of the pouncing wolf's head. The dead animal plopped onto the bed of fallen leaves and didn't move again. A third wolf attacked. This one's jaws clamped around Tony's forearm.

"Fuck!" Tony cried. "Goddamn it!"

Luca moved quickly. She pivoted and swatted the wolf across the snout with the flat side of her hatchet. It yelped and staggered off. Before it could attack again or retreat, I shoved Tony aside and shot the beast in the throat. Arterial spray showered the forest floor as the wolf danced the dance of the dying. I shot it again. It fell against a tree trunk and slid, lifeless, to the ground.

Something hit me hard and I lost my footing. When I struck the ground, I lost my breath. And the gun. My vision blurred. I tasted blood. Something was on top of me, something big, pinning me to the earth. I didn't know if it was wolf or man or something in between. All I knew was naked fear. Without my breath, I couldn't scream. Under this weight, I couldn't move. Something hot blew against the back of my neck. Wet drops of saliva soaked the back of my shirt. Air returned to my lungs, but all I could do was blubber as blackness swallowed me.

DOWN THE MOUNTAIN

I WOKE UP SURROUNDED BY the dead and in a fuck ton of pain. It was nearly morning. A sliver of orange flared in the eastern sky. The starry purple was retreating slowly. Clouds of fog clung to the surrounding trees. The air stunk of copper and piss and loosened bowels. My left shoulder blade stung most of all and my shirt around the injury was soaked with something sticky and warm. Luca and a wolf boy I assumed could only be Jonathan lay together in a tangle of bloody limbs. Her hatchet was buried in the side of his head. His hand, embedded in her chest. His closed eyes gave the illusion of peace despite the gory scene. Hers remained open and wide with terror of the void.

Several wolves lay about us. Some dead from gunshot wounds. Others torn open and hemorrhaging steaming piles of guts. I became aware of wet chewing sounds, like an oversized wad of gum in the mouth of hell. I tried to reorient myself. Tried to push myself to my hands and knees. The exertion was too much and I collapsed face-down again.

I managed to turn my head toward the awful chewing and almost vomited at the sight. Hank squatted among the shredded remains of Tony. My best friend's eyes stared sightlessly at me from his severed head. Hank had his mouth pressed to one of Tony's hands, eating it like fucking corn on the cob. Flecks of blood and ragged flaps of flesh fell between his hairy, clawed feet.

I had to get the fuck out of there.

Straining, I made my way to my hands and knees. Every muscle burned. I felt lightheaded. My breath came in and out in harsh, cool gasps. I pivoted and planted myself on my ass.

Hank turned to me and dropped Tony's mostly eaten hand. It landed with a sickening thump. He kept his teeth bared. Bloody drool fell from his heavily bearded chin. His eyes glowed that ghostly blue. The iciness of the stare stabbed into me like a knife left out in the snow. He stood. His pants had torn, and my gaze locked onto his massive, swinging wolf cock. That more than anything else made me panic.

I started sputtering pleas for mercy while simultaneously scanning the area for one of the rifles. He took a step forward, crinkling dead leaves. I scooted backwards, bumped a wolf corpse. My hand landed in a pile of guts. I gagged. Lifted my hand to look at it, now red and dripping with gristle. Hank took another step, this time snapping a twig.

Something in me snapped, too. I lurched to my feet. Grunted against the exquisite pain.

Where are the fucking guns?!

Hank came closer. A low growl rumbled in his throat. His hot breath made steam in the cool morning. I swore I could smell it: whiskey, dog breath, and rotted meat. Wet dog and unwashed man. His hands stretched out before him as he advanced. Hooked claws like cactus spines. The big wolf dick swung with each step, slapping his inner thighs.

I finally spotted one of the guns.

Behind him.

Fuck.

I held up my hands in a gesture of surrender.

"Hank, please. It's me."

He kept coming. Said nothing.

"Please, this isn't you. You've gotta fight it, man. Come on!"

His glowing wolf eyes narrowed into slits. He drew closer. So close now I could feel his goddamn body heat. A radiant cloud of foul humidity. Foul *humanity*. This wasn't some aberration, some anomaly of nature. This was Hank, the true Hank, the dormant beast, now awake, now hungry. I really needed to find that other gun.

A black and pink tongue licked across Hank's lips, across the points of his fangs.

"HANK!!!"

He was only a few paces from me now. He bent at the knees. Ready to pounce. Snarling, eyes burning, claws spread and reared back. I was a fucking goner.

Then an idea hit me.

I reached for my wounded shoulder blade. As I pressed my

fingers into the wet wound, I determined it was indeed a bite mark. Whether wolf or wolf man, I didn't know, but I had to try something. I smeared a generous amount of blood on my hand and reached out.

"I'm just like you," I said. "I'm a beast. I've been bitten. We're the same!"

Hank cocked his head to the side like a confused dog. He loosened. He still made his way toward me but at a more tentative pace. He leaned forward and sniffed my fingers.

"See. That's it. That's a good boy. I'm like you. We're the same. You don't have to . . . eat me." With my other hand, I reached for the buck knife at my hip. "That's a good boy." I let him lick the blood from my fingertips, then moved my hand to scratch behind his now pointed, leathery ear. He closed his eyes and leaned into the caress. "Yeah, see? That's right. It's okay."

I unsheathed the knife with a quickness I no longer thought myself capable of. He opened his eyes and snarled. Before he could bite my extended forearm, I rammed the blade under his chin. He gurgled and whined as hot blood spilled over my knife hand and pattered the ground between us. I shoved him away, removing the knife as I did so. He took three shaky steps backwards and collapsed in a heap.

The sky was nearly half-orange now. I turned back toward camp. While I ran, I kept the knife clutched tightly and pointed ahead. Ready to kill anything that got too close. Or die trying.

•••

I returned to camp and scared several carrion birds away from Bryan's corpse. One of his eyes was gone. The wound on his throat had been widened. Flies crawled and buzzed about him. They didn't scare as easily as the birds. I considered burying him. No time. The fire had gone out, so that was no use either. I had no choice but to leave him here. The birds would come back. I hoped there would be something left of him when the authorities came. Of course, I thought I might not even call anyone. I didn't know how to even begin explaining what happened. Save for writing it down, of course.

I gathered up some jerky and nuts and dried fruit, some water, and my notebook. I put it all in my backpack. I changed my clothes and did my best to clean myself up. When I felt I had everything I needed, I scoured the area for Tony's keys and hiked back down Moon Mountain, alone and in pain. Pointing the knife at shadows and sounds brought me brief moments of solace. But eventually, with only a third of the way to go, I tossed it away without a second thought. Something told me I wouldn't need it.

I reached the RV and leaned against it, pressing my forehead against the warm metal body. My breath slowed, grew steady. The bite on my shoulder blade didn't even hurt anymore.

•••

I drove Tony's RV to the outskirts of Paradise, parked it, and walked into town. I found a diner with chrome trim and dirty windows and booths that had housed some infinite amount of butts. The aroma of burnt coffee hung about the inside. Coffee sounded nice.

A blonde server with thick foundation and long, pink fingernails escorted me to a booth and handed me a menu. Not even ninety seconds later, she brought me black coffee. I ordered a hamburger and took out my notebook to start writing this manuscript you're now reading.

After Pink Fingernails poured me a refill on coffee, someone else walked through the door. The smell of a campfire clung to this new-comer so strongly it drew my attention to him. He dressed in a shiny, expensive looking suit. He had black hair, slicked back, and a white face so smooth it seemed he never had to shave. When he saw me, he grinned and a ball of lead filled my stomach.

He told Pink Fingernails he was here with me and approached my table and I didn't refute his claim as he slid in across from me. He ordered no food and no drink. He didn't even touch the ice water Pink Fingernails brought for him. We didn't speak. He'd say some-thing when he was ready, and I would listen. I knew that so deeply, I offered him no greeting, only continued writing, stopping to sip coffee every few minutes.

When my burger came out, he leaned forward. He zeroed in on me as I dressed the bun with ketchup and mayonnaise. As I dis-carded the onion and tomato and lettuce. As I lifted the sandwich to my lips.

I took one bite and gagged. I spit the bite onto the plate and lowered the sandwich.

He was grinning at me again.

I crossed my arms and leaned back. I stared into his black eyes.

"You have something to say?" I asked.

He maintained his grin for a beat, then spoke.

"You know who I am. You've heard what I can do. You know I can give you anything."

"Anything, huh?"

"Anything. You can kill Ayla without laying a finger on her. Get your boy back. Sober up, even. You just have to ask me, Walton."

"There's a catch," I said. "There always is."

"You'll live your life knowing you did something monstrous."

I touched my wounded shoulder blade. "I think I may become a monster regardless."

"Then what's the risk?"

I stared at him long and hard. The fiery smell was oppressive now, like I'd leaned my face near a campfire. I considered Mr. Boggs' words very carefully. Imagined Ayla dying. Imagined our son returning to me. Sobriety didn't seem so bad either. For some reason, I'd lost all urges to drink. I could have my boy back. I wasn't crazy about sacrificing Ayla. It seemed cruel and maybe even unnecessary. Of course, who knew what would happen, now with the wolf's blood running through me? How could I possibly return to normal life?

Pink Fingernails returned to the table.

"Are you gonna order anything?" she asked my well-dressed companion.

"I'm not sure yet."

With a subtle roll of her eyes, she looked at me. "Everything tasting okay, sir?"

I glanced down at my burger. I glanced at Mr. Boggs. "You know what? No. Not at all. I'm sorry. Here." I dug out a twenty and put it on the table. "I think I'll be moving on."

"Okay, you want change?"

"Keep it."

"Thank you." Everything about her brightened.

Cort Boggs watched me get up. As I turned, he said one final thing.

"You'll never get another chance," he said.

I didn't respond. I didn't even look back.

•••

I intended on returning to the RV. Driving until I found a police or sheriff's station. But a rustling sound in an alley gave me pause. I turned and saw a raccoon, digging in an overturned trashcan, eating the contents of a torn open bag. My own belly rumbled and I realized how hungry I was. The well-done burger at the diner had made me gag, but something about a fresh kill, even a verminous beast like a raccoon, made me salivate.

I walked toward the rodent. It didn't notice me. Only kept eating what looked like expired coleslaw. A growl started in my throat. I didn't even do it consciously.

I advanced on the creature, focused more on the hunt than on my hunger. I couldn't let my need distract me.

As I crept forward, I wondered what I'd do once I'd feasted. Once I'd fully embraced the animal. Shirked the man, the man who hadn't been much of a man to begin with.

The raccoon raised its face to me. Its black, cartoon criminal mask shadowed eyes filled with more curiosity than fear. It had nowhere to go. I was too close. *I will feed*, I thought. *And then I'll go home.*

Moon Mountain loomed ahead. The trees covering it swayed in the breeze. They seemed like a single great beast. A wolf-shaped cloud hovered over the snow-capped peak.

Yes. I'll go home.

THE VESSEL

MATT HARVEY

For Rachel Deering

Who I blame for getting me into this mess in the first place.

TWO HOODED FIGURES DRAGGED THE cradle into the room, announcing their arrival with the ear-piercing shriek of twisted metal grating on tile. The bearers were unfazed by the cacophony, but it was all Annika could do to stop from wincing at the sound. The battered wreck of a thing was metal interwoven with an ink-black, viscous material that shuddered at the touch, undulating like something alive. The material's elasticity was the only thing holding the cradle together, and only just.

"The Atramentium you see here,"—the Elder gestured to the bizarre substance—"sustains our master between hosts. Sadly, little of it remains. Over the decades we have failed him. He has managed to subsist upon it, but it grows scarce. I fear the next failure may be our last." He waited for the gravity of his words to sink in and for the scraping to subside. The cradle now in place, the comparative quiet gave his words the emphasis he sought. "And that is why *we must not fail.*"

She watched the Elder and the macabre tableau before her in disbelief. This was nothing like she had imagined when she joined the Heralds of Celestial Ascendancy. She'd come so far, but now, every thought and every muscle screamed at her to run, leave this circle, strip off this flowing robe embroidered with arcane, unknowable symbols, get out of this house, get into her car, and get as far away from this as possible. In her thoughts, Annika could almost hear the words she wanted to scream, but she was unable to give them a voice. If she could have, they would have been something along the lines of, "I only came here because I wanted what everyone wants: To serve a higher purpose, to know my place in the universe. I did *not* sign up for this."

Panic was rising in her chest, but she could only force herself to gulp shallow breaths. As much as she needed to catch her breath, she was trying desperately to avoid inhaling the overpowering stench of decay hanging in the air. Her eyes darted around the room nervously for somewhere to run, but instead they found the Elder. Somehow he had silently arrived at her side. He placed his hand on her shoulder, and it felt solid—weighty and reassuring. She felt rooted to the spot by it. Almost against her will, she turned to see his wizened face and calm, steady eyes. He looked at her for a moment without speaking and she felt as though the world had stopped spinning.

After an instant that felt like an eternity, she let out a long, deep breath, and the panic drifted out of her with it. Whatever doubts had seized her passed, and the Elder turned his attention back to the corpse in the center of the room.

"Now it begins."

Slowly, the assembled Heralds of Celestial Ascension began to speak. Some of the neophytes mumbled haltingly at first, as the words were strange and hard to master. But as they repeated them, they grew strong and clear.

Ek Mynehli Shabba Kekh—Emerge!

Venth Mynehli Eb Supptu Kekh—Emerge!

Venth Nahi

Venth Ypskellum

Venth Inkhum

Emerge!

With each repetition Annika's tongue wrapped itself around the strange words more and more adeptly, her voice merging with the others, the chant filling her with a calm openness. Their voices coalesced into one, and with each repetition, she felt herself slipping away, being subsumed by the words. "Love is letting go," the Elder had told her—letting go of expectations, of the ego, of the person she had been to embrace a truer reality—something deep and important. Whatever barely remembered doubts she had completely evaporated. All that remained was a warm, enveloping haze that was as close to love as she had ever experienced.

At her feet was the cause of her fading apprehensions, a naked cadaver, once a pretty brunette, trim and tall. Now her skin was a glacial blue, her eyes yellowing, pupils occluded with a milky glaze. Those dead, dull eyes gazed emptily up at nothing, oblivious to the figures that encircled their corpse and watched over it for the better part of a day. None of them looked at the dead woman's eyes though—they watched her abdomen. Something was moving inside her, sending spasmodic ripples fluttering across her bluing flesh. At last, their Master was stirring.

All at once, from within the corpse's thorax came a wet, gurgled chomp. The body's lower half convulsed fitfully, legs twitching in a flurry of spasms. The chewing became more insistent, each bite accompanied by an oozing, billowing motion across the dead woman's stomach, like watching a ripple across a lake from underwater. Her corpse twitched more and more violently now, threshing in mute convulsions. The legs splayed out in unnatural angles, and the bones snapped with a sound like twigs trampled underfoot as the contortions whiplashed through her extremities.

The carcass's legs having been wrenched sufficiently akimbo, the thrashing ceased. Before long, a moist sucking sound emanated from the corpse's distended abdomen, a gurgling, gagging swallow of some foul-smelling fluid. Then, all at once, a gush of blackened ooze erupted with tremendous force from between the body's legs, spurting through the birth canal like an aberrant mockery of a pregnant woman's water breaking. This deluge of filth was followed by a wet, belching slosh. After the initial ejaculation, the foul-hued gunk continued to leak slowly from between her splattered thighs, dripping onto the floor and filling the room with an overpowering reek. Warm and acidic, the smell was of something older and more wretched than decay. The gnawing continued to increase in volume as their Master drew closer, bite following bite more rapidly, gnashing toward a repugnant crescendo. The sounds of splintering bone and cartilage filled the room and one of the neophytes dropped their corner of the cradle and vomited. As the malodorous atmosphere and nerve-wracking clangor of the chewing reached an intolerable zenith, the corpse's pelvis burst open with a final, wrenching creak. Shards of bone, sinew, and a torrent of polluted blood, sultry with the remnants of the black ooze, sprayed all over the room. The cradle and the remaining neophyte bearing it were drenched in the thick, syrupy fluid, and the one who vomited fainted dead away in a corner, collapsing into the puddle of still-warm sick at their feet.

The flesh that remained of the corpse's pelvis, blossomed like the petals of some hideous, malformed flower, was hanging on the shards of the ilia, glistening with blood befouled by the black secretion. It dripped from the shredded cartilage and sinew like morning dew on blades of grass. From this gore-soaked aperture, the Master of these hooded devotees finally emerged. For some of them, this was their first time laying eyes upon the creature. Whatever they were told to expect was insufficient to prepare them.

A slithering, seeping obsidian mass wriggled into sight, formless and hungry. The amorphous thing was barbed with jagged outcroppings of teeth. The teeth were yellowed, craggy shapes ringed with black filth, caked with blood, and wreathed by shreds of flesh. At its shambolic approach, the Atramentium of the cradle pulsated, as if calling to it. The cradle lay not six feet away, but the creature oozed across the floor toward it at a maddeningly slow rate. The Heralds had awaited the coming of a thing to be worshipped and instead beheld a sickly abomination, enfeebled from decades without a viable host. One of the acolytes moved to help it to its goal, but the Elder raised a cautionary hand.

"The Master is strong enough."

The figures watched intently as the shape crept across the floor, wrenching itself inexorably on. After what seemed an eternity, it reached the cradle at last, becoming almost indistinguishable from the black sheen of the Atramentium that ran through it. The lid of the battered structure, twisted and nearly pulverized into uselessness, improbably managed to slam shut with a shuddering thud. Their Master was safe again. It would contract in its cradle until it was a tiny thing, small enough to enter a new vessel unseen and insidious, and the cycle would begin anew.

The devotees of the black shape let out a collective sigh of relief, save for the weak-stomached one lying in the corner, his barely audible groans forgotten for the moment.

•••

Elise Abbington bolts upright, waking from a nightmare. She's sweating in the cool air of the April night, her blinking eyes scanning the pitch-black bedroom, looking for a landmark, something . . . anything familiar. Then, all at once, something throbs through her, blotting out every other sensation except the flashes of white heat bursting in her eyes. Her head hangs down, loose strawberry-blonde hair falling onto her freckled shoulders as she catches her breath. She considers waking Peter, but that would be silly.

Wouldn't it?

"This is going to go away," she thinks, "it's going to stop any moment now." But it continues, louder, deeper, more insistent. She tries to listen, to see where this is coming from, but it's everywhere at once. Then, her ears pop painfully hard, and now it's not dull, not distant. She's suddenly gripped by a horrible thought, "It's coming from inside me. There's something inside me making this unbearable noise."

Her heart races, quickening with the pulse of something *other* that's running through her veins. This is nothing like when she was pregnant with Eliott, this is something else entirely. An invader, a parasite—something awful. Beneath the pulsing is another sound, fainter but growing with each deafening surge—a thousand multiplying whispers, hissing and wailing, throbbing in one ear and then the other, oscillating faster and faster, torment in stereo. The pitch of the voices grows higher and higher until it's a single, deafening shriek shooting through her body. Her vision goes completely white and she clutches the sheets so hard her nails tear through them, digging into her palms. Elise's muscles tighten around her spine, like a thousand violin strings wound too tight. Not that she'd notice, but she hasn't dared to breathe.

Before the pounding in her body becomes too great to bear and the white-hot noise threatens to engulf her completely, it stops. At last, she lets a ragged, feral gasp out, like the revenant of a trapped scream escaping the cage of her chest. Beads of sweat drop from her brow, spattering the torn sheets below, and she sits gasping in the stillness, utterly drained. She stares at the intermittent white flashes before her eyes until they grow so infrequent as to be gone entirely. How long it's taken she's not sure, but she's breathing normally again. She turns to see Peter lying on his side, facing away from her and snoring, blissfully unaware. Which is typical. She would smile, but she's too exhausted.

She staggers to the bathroom and leans shakily in front of the mirror, splashing her face with cold water. By the time she looks up at her reflection, the whole thing is already fading away—the nightmare, the migraine, the panic attack, whatever that was. She looks at the stainless-steel fixtures of the sink, the polished tile, the neatly arranged razors and electric toothbrushes. All these things that make this place hers, the creams and lotions lined up like rows of little soldiers keeping silent vigil over the placid order of her countertop, her home, her world. She sees everything is in its place. Everything is normal. The world makes sense.

The smile finally comes, and she chuckles to herself. Maybe she'll tell her therapist about this next week, but more than likely, she'll go back to sleep and forget it ever happened.

•••

"Elise? Elise, honey? It's 7:45 already. We gotta *move!*" Peter is waking her up, which *never* happens. She's running late, and of course Peter has screwed up Eliott's lunch. She's more disoriented than angry—after all he's trying to help—but it's another thing she has to do before work. Her embattled husband serves their son burnt scrambled eggs (How did he manage to burn scrambled eggs?) in a flurry of poorly coordinated motion. He's somehow transformed cooking breakfast into a Keystone Cops routine. "I tried to wake you up, but you wouldn't budge."

"Yeah, I—" She thinks about telling him what happened, but Eliott's listening, and kids don't need to hear about their parents' nightmares, so she improvises. "I think I slept on my neck weird." And that's as far as it goes because Peter has to catch the train into the city and it doesn't seem like such a big deal anyway. On the way to drop Eliott off at school, she absently listens to him chattering in the passenger seat—he has to pick a president to do a report on.

"Teddy Roosevelt's mustache is cool, what about him?"

"Well, I mean, he was a eugenicist, so there's that."

"A you-what? Is that bad?"

"Yeah, buddy. It's definitely bad. Then there's the whole Rough Riders, I mean . . ." There was a time when she could decry American colonialism with very specific examples, but today nothing comes to her, and she doesn't have the energy to be very convincing.

"Rough riders? They sound awesome! I'm gonna change it in my report and say they rode dinosaurs. Then Mrs. Williams will *have to* give me an A."

•••

In the ensuing days, Elise loses herself in the warm, numbing blur of normalcy. Her work, his work. Are her designs for the new winery's campaign going to be approved? Is Peter's department going to merge with accounts? Is Teddy Roosevelt's mustache, in fact, "cool?" What restaurant are they going to for date night? The *Weekly* said the new Italian place is really good, but he wants Thai, and she doesn't care as long as they have wine. That voice in the night is a phantom now, a dimly remembered moment of turbulence in the long, smooth voyage of their well-adjusted lives. The world, it seems, *does* make sense.

For a while.

She's outside Eliott's karate class a few evenings later, watching with a few other parents who arrived early to pick their kids up. On the other side of the glass, the boys and girls go through their stances, eyes intent, faces impossibly earnest. Her son is an orange belt and very proud of it. Next to her is the mother of Eliott's friend Sam, who she's met several times at various kids' birthday parties, but she studiously avoids any line of conversation that would require her to remember this woman's name, which is something like Amanda or maybe Amelia? Amandamelia, however, likes to talk. As she prattles on, Elise sizes her up: bottle-blonde and too skinny, but she begrudgingly acknowledges this woman is conventionally pretty, something like a Fox News anchor. Elise can imagine her suggesting re-reading *The Secret* at her weekly books-and-mimosas club. She's harmless enough, but she just *keeps* talking.

". . . So, Principal Koski and I, we have the same esthetician. She was getting a perm last week, and my first thought was, *Who still gets perms?* But anyway, I thought to myself, screw parent-teacher meetings. I've got a captive audience. So I gave her my elevator pitch."

Elise realizes it's her turn to prompt AmandaAnnikaAmelia to continue. It doesn't take much, just a mumbled, "Uh-huh."

"These kids, they're gonna get into trouble. I mean, they're kids, it's what they do, right? But detention doesn't help. I used to be a teacher's aide, before Trevor made partner, and trust me, nobody likes it—teachers, kids, *nobody*. So I said, why not try meditation? That's what these kids need to learn to keep them out of trouble in the first place—mindfulness. I was reading about it in the *Atlantic*. Apparently, they do it in Finland and it totally works."

Elise wants to disagree because she generally disagrees with this woman as a concept, but in all honesty, she can't. And the fact this sounds like a non-awful idea somehow makes Amandannikamelia even more annoying. She mutters something like an assent and looks down at her phone, trying to find a client's email important enough to disentangle her from this conversation.

"I mean, it could be a *game-changer*, you know?"

Elise smiles a smile that hopefully means whatever this woman wants to hear and watches her son practicing his kicks through the window. But, of course, she keeps talking. As Elise tries to tune what's-her-name's voice out, white flashes begin to cloud her vision. She blinks to shake them off, but they keep getting worse. Then sounds start to dissolve, becoming indistinguishable overlapping noises scraping painfully through her ears. Soon even that fades, and all that remains is a dull echo, steadily thrumming. Elise's chest gets so tight she could swear her heart's stopped. And then she realizes, she knows that sound. She's heard it before, the echo of a nightmare she told herself she'd forgotten.

The slow, rhythmic thudding pulses through her veins in the regular tempo of a heartbeat, growing slowly, inevitably louder. And then the whine of the discordant voices fades in beneath it and her vision goes white and she *remembers*. She's leaning forward, trying to catch her breath, her sweaty palm slipping down the glass when Sam's mom finally notices something's wrong. Elise feels her shuddering knees about to give out from under her and the only coherent thought she can form is, "*Please* don't pass out on the street in front of Annalyssamelia or whoever this bitch is." The kids run out from class in a cascade of noise and a blur of hands and feet and colorful belts. She closes her eyes for a moment and Eliott is hugging her and everything is back to normal. Sam's mom wants to make sure she's okay and Eliott wants to know if she saw how high he was kicking and of course the answer to both things is, "Yeah, of course," and a smile she hopes doesn't look as forced as it feels.

Sam's mom looks at her with a caring, almost motherly smile that says, *I know what you're going through, girlfriend.* Elise feels the words *yeah right, bitch* form and die on her tongue and instead keeps screwing her face in what she hopes is the shape of a reassuring smile in return. As Sam starts tugging at her jacket to leave because he was apparently promised ice cream, his mother still somehow finds time to give Elise one last piece of unsolicited advice.

"Elise, pardon me for saying this but, you look dehydrated. I know it sounds crazy, but that raw juicing article I recommended from *Buzzfeed*, it's totally—"

"A game-changer. Yeah. You know, the way I feel right now, I probably should check it out. You guys have a good night.

"Good night, Sam," Elise adds, trying to sound more cheery, and Eliott echoes her and then proceeds to demonstrate the blocks he's working on for his purple belt while reciting a litany of martial arts weapons he wants for his birthday. Elise laughs weakly because she's too tired to explain why a katana is not an appropriate gift for a nine-year-old and because, if she didn't, she would probably break down in tears.

•••

The next day after lunch, Elise lets her co-workers Michelle and Bryant go on ahead of her on their way back to the office. She detours into the drugstore and peruses the endless array of lipsticks, even though she doesn't need any. And even though she *knows* it's stupid, she walks down the "Family Planning" aisle. She's not pregnant. Of course she isn't—she's got an IUD—but she can't shake the feeling there's something else inside her body, whatever it was that woke her up in the night a week ago, that almost brought her to her knees in front of the dojo last night.

"You finding everything okay?"

Elise starts, shaken from contemplating the various scenarios that could have resulted in an unplanned pregnancy.

"Do you need help finding anything?" asks the middle-aged woman, Doreen, according to her name-tag. Doreen looks at Elise guilelessly, with understanding, sympathy even, and she doesn't know why, but it disgusts her. She's not pregnant, and this is stupid.

She mumbles, "No thanks," and sets the lipstick down clumsily, knocking over a pile of bright-purple packs of maxi-pads. Elise hurriedly leaves the store. It takes every ounce of her willpower to stop from running.

•••

Three nights later, her period comes, announcing itself with brutal cramps and a ripping headache, and of course, it arrives the night before her revisions for the winery campaign are due. But fake-smiling her way through the next day is a little easier because at least she *knows*. She knows she's not pregnant. She spends the last couple of hours in her office googling migraine symptoms and trying without success to get them to match what she's been feeling. Even so, the warm, messy tide of blood between her legs is a relief. She celebrates with four glasses of wine at dinner and sleeps almost as easily as Peter that night.

•••

"Regular coffee for Hicks?"

"That's me." Edgar Hicks, six feet and two inches of lanky weather-beaten Kentuckian, smiles politely as he takes his coffee from the skinny, dreadlocked barista with a prominent pin on her apron reading "SUPPORT YOUR LOCAL COVEN." She's a prime reminder why he hates towns like this: smug enclaves of entitlement with boutique downtown shops, artisanal gastropubs, wine bars, and a placid river dribbling through downtown. As he sits outside The Bean Scene ("Purveyors of Ethically-Sourced, Locally-Inspired Caffeine and Love," according to their bullshit-ass sign) sipping a six-dollar cup of coffee, he can't help but think about how many kids from towns like this he's found—a thousand miles from home, blank-eyed, strung-out, taken by another snake-oil salesman with a nose for trust funds and cocaine. How many dumb motherfucking kids has he fished out of rivers like the one running through this town?

He's joined in short order by Ruben, a thirty-four-year-old Hispanic man who despite having a wrestler's frame, looks like an IT guy. "Good coffee here, am I right?" Hicks nods because, despite the ethical sourcing and local inspiration, the coffee is shitty. "So, uh, Mr. Hicks, I've been dying to ask you . . . How did you get into this line of work?"

"I don't like bullshit, kid."

Ruben waits patiently for a further explanation that is not

forthcoming. He's taken aback by Hicks' bluntness, as are most people who meet the man. Even at fifty-three years old, Hicks looks like the wrong person to fuck with. For the past thirty years, he's been tracking down people's children (and occasionally parents) and bringing them home from places like The Exalted Peak of Knowledge, The New Home of Christ on Earth, and Eternity's Doorstep. He'd seen sun-worshippers, moon-worshippers, animal-worshippers, incestuous Christian communes, cannibals, houngans, child sacrifice, and even a group that thought JFK was the second coming of Jesus himself. But behind every curtain, there was always just another little man (or every so often, a woman) pulling the levers to get the same old shit—money, power, sex.

Ruben feels compelled to move whatever-this-is along in the hopes of arriving somewhere in the neighborhood of a conversation. "So, you must like it. Being a deprogrammer, I mean."

"Yeah. I get to help a lot of people." Now Hicks is the one bullshitting. Helping people was part of it, but mostly that was a stock response and sounded good to clients. His own personal brand of bullshit is probably the only kind Hicks couldn't recognize. Despite his generally unpleasant demeanor, he truly does love his job. Deprogramming brought order to the world around him—a world of bullshitters and the bullshitted.

"I bet. I mean, I wish I had your number last year. Before my step-brother, Ignacio, got mixed up in all this craziness."

"I heard about him. My condolences. The Heralds don't fuck around."

"I promised myself at his funeral I would find those bastards."

Ruben looks away now because, even a year later, he still tears up at the memory of watching his step-brother's casket descend into the earth, watching his parents' hearts break and seeing Ignacio's kids' world shattered. Hicks didn't seem like the kind of guy to pour your heart out to. After a moment's silence, Ruben turns back to him. "And then I found Lawrence. And I found you."

"We're gonna get 'em kid. As long your man on the inside, Larry, doesn't fuck up or fuck us over, we're gonna nail these sons of bitches." Hicks grunts a reply. After a moment, he offers, "Look, I know what it's like." He takes another sip of the shitty coffee. "With brothers. I deprogrammed mine a long time ago."

Ruben leans in, surprised, eager to hear more. "Wait, what?"

"Kid, if bullshit was wine, I'd be a master sommelier. I got a taste for it young. My daddy was a preacher—handled snakes, spoke in tongues, laid hands, exorcised demons. In a word, the man was a bullshitter." Hicks pauses here, his eyes scanning the passersby keenly. "And people loved him for it."

"So you . . ." Ruben's question tails off for fear of overstepping the man's boundaries.

"Yeah. The first person I ever deprogrammed was myself. That broke Mawmaw's heart, but when I came back for my brother, that shattered the Church, which shattered the family." Hicks looks absently in his jacket pocket for cigarettes and realizes in frustration he was currently "quitting." So with nothing to put in his mouth to shut him up, he adds a final thought. "But it was worth it."

And Hicks believes this with an almost religious fervor. It had been worth seeing Mawmaw wailing on her knees, begging God for mercy in the middle of town, screaming over his daddy's dead body because Hicks got to live in a world that *made sense*. And it kept making sense, for a long time . . . until about three years ago.

That schism in the order of his world brought him here, despite not having much to go on. He knows, somewhere in this pretentiously unpretentious corner of Northern California, amid the Bay Area exburbs filled with software developers trying to escape their miserable grinds, the thing he sought is waiting. It is here and it is growing—gestating and squirming inside one of these yoga-practicing, soy latte-sipping, soul-cycling idiot's bodies. He doesn't know exactly where yet, but he's going to find it and he's going to excise it and kill it before it can grow. Here, in Sonoma County, California, he is going to end this.

"Look, the Elder doesn't know I'm here, but that's gonna change soon. They know my face. They know yours, Ruben?"

"No, not that I know of anyway." He's trying to sound reassuring and failing miserably.

"Well, Larry sure as hell does." Hicks scans Ruben's face as if looking for the weakest spot to strike and, with one barb or revelation, send all of Ruben's hopes for revenge and redemption tumbling down like a stack of cards. Hicks can tell Ruben is a smart kid, probably a lot smarter than he is, but he's confident he knows better in one important area: Survival. Ruben breaks his gaze and glanced at his phone for the hundredth time, and for the hundredth time, there's nothing. It's a stupid risk, Hicks knows, sitting here in this coffee shop and watching. After all, they *know his face*. Abruptly, he rises from his seat. "Come on, kid, this coffee fucking sucks."

Ruben, feeling out of his depth, follows the older man to his auburn 1974 Malibu.

•••

Hicks sits on the edge of the sagging mattress in his room at the Super Value 101 Motor Lodge, methodically sipping Wild Turkey and taking inventory as he does every day. It's his ritual. It had been a long time since he'd left the church, but he grew up with ritual, and he remained a man of ritual in spite of himself. Handcuffs. Pepper spray. Brass Knuckles. Ibuprofen. Binoculars. Beretta M9A1. Burner phone. Sig Sauer P226 MK-25. Ammo. Duct tape. Flashlight. 12" Tactical Bowie knife. .44 Magnum. More ammo. The tools of his trade spread out on a grease-smeared terry-cloth towel, he cleans his guns, half-listening to the Weather Channel, and he and Ruben wait.

Ruben shifts awkwardly in his seat, trying to break the stifling, awkward silence Hicks is somehow perfectly content with. "So, how did you first run into the Heralds? What was that like?"

Hicks doesn't look up from his guns and doesn't much feel like talking, but the words seem to come out unbidden, like the story itself wants to be told, despite the reticence of the storyteller. "About three years ago, I met a Dr. and Mrs. Dwight Emerson. Their little chip-off-the-ol'-block, Dwight Jr., fit the profile of most of my clientele: rich, white, from a good family. Junior, it seemed, had dropped out of Brown to join a commune—imagine the scandal! What would Dr. Emerson tell his golf buddies?

"In point of fact, the venerable Doctor and Mrs. Emerson had no earthly idea what their boy had gotten into. Junior had joined the Heralds of Celestial Ascendancy, a small, obscure sect that worshipped a . . . *thing* they believed came from outer space. He left everything behind to travel 'round the country, trying to find it a viable human female host so it could fulfill its destiny of . . . well, that part still ain't clear. Every host, every *vessel* as they refer to them, has died. It ain't even close to the craziest "religion" I've encountered by a long ways. But there was a catch. The creature they worship . . . I seen it, and what's worse, I smelled it."

"So you mean . . . what you're saying is . . . ?" Is all Ruben manages to stammer out.

"This ain't another meth-fueled preacher hocking universal consciousness to find his seventh wife. What these people worship . . . it's real." What Hicks doesn't say is that the object of their worship being real scares the ever-loving shit out of him.

Luckily, Ruben says it for him. "If that's true, that's some scary shit, man."

Hicks looks up from a disassembled handgun to add, "The Heralds shootin' my ass and forcing my '69 Super Bee off the side of a god-damned mountain wasn't reassuring neither." Despite the steel rod the doctors put in his left leg after they scraped him off the side of a West Virginia highway, Hicks is still chasing that thing, just in a '74 Malibu these days. He doesn't know exactly why, but he can sense the shape of his reasons as clear as he can feel the winter in the bar in his leg.

That jet-black thing he'd seen slithering across the floor cracked the windshield of his worldview, and we all know how that ends: the crack keeps spider-webbing across the surface until the whole thing collapses. It can take a while, but that's how it *always* ends.

He snuffed out whatever faith his daddy beat into him long ago. He couldn't go through life on his knees, a little boy squealing when the belt landed across his backside. Hicks tells himself he tore down the walls of his father's church because what they worshipped wasn't real—and it wasn't—but that wasn't why. Not *really*. Somewhere beneath the booze and the scars and the years of unmasking innumerable false gods, the real reason is still down there. He caught a glimpse of it when he saw that filthy black shape ooze across the floor in Barboursville, West Virginia and finally found a God that existed. One look at that thing and he was the person he vowed *never* to be again—a scared kid cowering before the supernatural. Somewhere in the back of his mind Hicks mulls this over as he loads his pistols. It isn't a coherent thought, maybe not even a feeling, but it's there.

Hicks raises the plastic motel cup of whiskey to his lips and Ruben's phone vibrates. Finally.

"Lawrence, talk to me."

"I have some pictures for you. A body in a house out in Bodega Bay. I don't know if it's still there, but I'll text you the address. I gotta go."

•••

A few minutes later, Lawrence hands the Elder his phone, and he takes it awkwardly, regarding it like something alien and strange. "It's already dialing, just—" The old man sneers at him and the sentence dies before it's complete.

"Lawrence?" Guillermo, the voice on the other end answers.

"No. This is the Elder."

"Oh, I'm sorry Exalted One, it's just . . . Lawrence's name came up on my caller ID and—"

"No matter. Someone is there. Someone knows. Whatever you're doing, do it faster."

"Y-y-yes, of course," the voice stammers.

"I want to know who's watching us." He smacks his dry lips, the next words forming a disagreeable taste on them. "Especially if it's Hicks."

"Hicks? Is he— I mean—"

The Elder disdainfully hands Lawrence back his phone and Lawrence, trying to distract himself from shitting bricks and the questions racing through his mind, wonders "How did the Elder already know they were being watched? How much does he know? Is this a test? Is he trying to catch me red-handed and giving me more rope to string myself up with? Is Hicks working with Ruben?" He instead forces himself to reflect that this aging, brittle man is more comfortable with things from beyond this earth than with an iPhone.

Lawrence leaves the room in a hurry, leaving the Elder to relish a rare moment of solitude. He sinks down in the leather chair of his library, his body at last fully exhaling. The tension leaves his shoulders, his frame shrivels, revealing its antiquity. He sighs wearily, looking down at the same book that's been in front of him for years— his bible, his North Star—the *Astronomicon*, as he's come to call it. He doesn't know its real title, and the vast majority of its contents he cannot read. Its mystery has consumed him as surely as his age. His bony hand kneads a brow furrowed under the weight of the decades he's spent chasing this knowledge. Alone in his sanctum, he allows himself the momentary weakness of feeling the full burden of his destiny. He feels the onus of his followers' faith, along with all he's endured: the lives taken, the miles traveled, and the frustrations of a litany of failures. His eyes close and he breathes deeply for a time, (Minutes? Hours?) until a rapping sounds on the heavy door, as it always inevitably does. He pulls himself back, sets his shoulders, and blinks his sparkling eyes alert and ready. The Elder has returned.

"Come in."

"I've seen her," Annika enthuses as she enters, eyes alight with hope. Despite having this conversation many, many times before, the Elder can't help but smile. This belief, the unshakable call to destiny, she believes it so purely, and her belief feeds his, just as his belief kindled hers when she came to him months ago. "She's perfect."

"Child, our destiny demands a heavy burden upon you." She approaches his desk hesitantly, unsure of how much eagerness she should betray. The Elder takes her hands in his and gazes directly into her green eyes. The openness with which they return his gaze stirs something within him. A memory now, but if he was twenty years younger . . . "I need you to watch over her. Stay close to her."

"Of course. Her boy, Eliott, he has a playdate with my Sam this weekend. I'll make sure we get some quality time."

"Good, good," he replies absently, the words drifting unhurriedly from between his weathered lips. Neither of them seem to notice how long the Elder keeps caressing her well-manicured hand, both of them lost in their own private fantasies; his of what would have been in the past, hers of what may yet be in the future.

Ruben watches Hicks like a hawk. The man never seems to stop drinking. "How do you do that? All day, I mean." Hicks doesn't respond, he just keeps leafing through the pictures Ruben got Lawrence, periodically raising the flask to his lips. Ruben looks over Hicks' shoulder and sees the image of a woman's corpse, her legs splayed and wrenched apart to reveal a gruesome aperture wet with blood and something black and foul. Atramentium, Hicks calls it.

"It makes it easier to look at this shit." Hicks' words hang there for a moment, neither man having much to add. "We're close, kid. You're sure nobody saw you at the house?"

"Yeah. I'm sure."

"When are you meeting Larry in-person again? We need to know where this thing is going to be implanted next."

"It's already done. These pics are a couple weeks old now. There wasn't much at the house. I told him—" A knock at the door interrupts Ruben.

Hicks shoves him aside roughly and produces a pistol in one swift motion. "And I told *you*," he hisses through gritted teeth, "you don't ever tell your source where the fuck we're staying."

Ruben edges toward the door, hands up, and whispers, "Hicks, fucking chill, man." The look on Hicks' face however, is decidedly not fucking chill. Not fucking chill in the slightest. The fact he's brandishing a loaded weapon isn't particularly reassuring either. Ruben cocks his eyebrow and whispers again: "Fucking. Chill."

He opens the door, interposing his body between it and Hicks, takes the Chinese food from the delivery kid, and makes sure to tip twenty percent. He spreads out the food on the table. Hicks flicks the safety back on and puts the gun on the dresser. "I told him we'd meet tomorrow."

"We?" Ruben asks.

"Yeah, that was the condition. He needed to know I was serious. You're something of a celebrity in their circle, apparently. I'm not important enough to talk to."

"But you confirmed it?"

"Yes. They have a new vessel, and she's here." After Hicks doesn't reply, he adds, "In town," and immediately feels stupid for doing so.

Ruben can't help hoping Hicks will thank him, even sarcastically.

Instead, between bites, Hicks grunts, "You didn't tell him about your dead step-brother?" Ruben shoves a plastic forkful of chow mein in his mouth rather than answer. "Makes sense," Hicks continues, now speaking to nobody in particular. Better they don't know it's personal. Pass the fucking mu shu pork."

•••

"Please sit down, I was just pouring myself a glass of wine and . . . oopsy, I poured two." Elise is sitting in Annika's living room, which she begrudgingly admits is really nice. Sleek and modern but with enough plants and books to feel organic and welcoming. She makes a mental note to compliment her on the Ai WeiWei lithograph. Eliott and Sam are already upstairs whooping over the noise of the PS4.

"Thanks, Annika." Annika. She learned the woman's name at last when she heard her instruct Eliott not to call her "Mrs. Schofield." She's forcefully inserted it into their conversation now in the hopes she won't forget it. The wine is good, and she's in no hurry this particular night. Peter already texted her during his layover in Denver, which was mercifully brief, because Elise is too protective of his ego to tell him how much she relishes his business trips. Besides, he had been asking her strange questions. He'd noticed a change in her and was concerned, which she resents. She hasn't felt this good in years, and here was her husband, urging her to see a doctor? It's a moot point anyway, because after this very nice Petit Sirah and a quick drive home, Elise will have the house to herself for at least one peaceful night.

"Hey, Annika, I—" She did it again. Hopefully it doesn't feel as unnatural to hear as it does to say. "I wanted to apologize for the other night at the dojo. I know I was a little short, it's just . . ." She realizes she hasn't planned for the end of the sentence and nothing reasonable is coming to her.

"Don't even think twice about it." Annika is right next to her now, and she takes Elise's hand, which is less startling than she thought it would have been. "I could see you had something going on. We've all been there." There's a pause and a smile now, a pleasing rhythm that along with the wine and the thought of the house to herself and her new vibrator seems to take the tension out of Elise's shoulders. "But, now . . . you're looking *great*. You're glowing."

Elise feels herself blush a little and smiles as she takes a drink of the wine because Annika's right—she feels *good*, better than she has in a long time. Her skin has cleared up, her hair is shiny without putting anything in it, and her allergies have been conspicuously absent. Most of all though, it's nice that *someone* noticed.

173

Friday
11 PM to MIDNITE

the VESSEL

"Say hello to the cult next door."

THIS MOVIE MAY NOT BE
APPROPRIATE FOR ALL VIEWERS
DISCRETION IS ADVISED

CHANNEL
83
WGHP

420 MOVIE—Comedy; 2 hrs. ★
"King Bong Tokes Manhattan." (1979)
New York City is terrorized by a monstrous marijuana water pipe. Government
blames radioactive hippies.

2 **6** **11** MONSTER M*A*S*H; 30 min.
The Transylvanian War rages on. Dracul-
eye gets busted drinking from one of his
patients. "Cold Lips" Ghoulihan and Fran-
kenburns stake his tent, with a plot to
bring his shenanigans to light. (Repeat)

VTV HEAVY METAL VIDEOS; 24 hrs.
Host Harvey Matthews counts down the
top heavy metal hits.

12 AM **83** MOVIE—Horror; 2 hrs. ★★★
"The Vessel." (1986) A religious deprogrammer travels to California to stop an
ancient cult from resurrecting their dark
lord. Californians are too high to notice.

SPORTS
SATURDAY/*Continued from page 50*
HEADLESS HORSE RACING 7 PM (KSN)
Bleeders' Crown Series finals.
CANNIBALL 9 PM (EZPN)
Xenia Xombies at Vancouver Vamps
SHLOCCER 10 PM (KIK)
Hurled Cup Semifinals - Zanzibar vs Iceland

"I'm gonna have another glass. Do you want one? I know you gotta drive, but . . ." Elise pinches the air to indicate "a little one" and giggles. Annika giggles back. There's a moment when she wonders, with a little bit of trepidation, are they becoming gal-pals?

Annika triple-checks the lock on the door from the kitchen to the garage on her way back. She wants to open the door and look at the body that's wrapped up there almost as much as she wants to keep Elise near her as long as possible. Somehow knowing that Peter's decapitated corpse is so close to his wife makes the whole experience electrifying. She feels giddy, like a teenager on a first date. She composes herself in the kitchen, and then returns to Elise with the bottle and, of course, pours her a full glass and then some.

"I'm glad to see you feeling better. I've been on kind of a high lately too, and I want everyone to be as excited about the future as I am." This is the part, Elise realizes, where she's supposed to prod the conversation forward. A raise of the eyebrow is all that's needed. "I've never been like, *religious*, but I always considered myself to be *spiritual*, you know? And I've been getting into this group that talks about mankind's place in the cosmos and where we're headed and it's been so fulfilling. I'm like, so torn between wanting to shout it from the mountaintop and also not talk everyone's ear off about it."

And just like that, Elise is completely relieved of any desire to become gal-pals with this woman. "What did I get myself into with that second glass of wine?" she thinks. All she can think of as a response is, "Huh."

Thankfully, Sam calls, "Mom!" from upstairs and the opportunity to escape presents itself. By the time Annika comes back Elise has finished the wine and is "on the phone with a client." She excuses herself and is out the door, but Annika insists on getting a last salvo of small-talk in.

"Elise, promise me you'll be careful, okay? If anything happened to you, I would just . . ." she pauses, and Elise is incredibly uncomfortable, because Annika looks like she's about to cry. Elise stands there, trying to be patient and Annika finally stammers, "I'd never forgive myself."

Elise forces the words, "Aren't you sweet," out of her mouth and follows it with, "But really . . . it was just two glasses of wine, I'm fine."

Annika's expression is fixed in concern and affection, like a mother sending her kid off for the first day of school. Elise can't decide if it's creepy or pathetic or just odd. Maybe she's drunk? "Just take care, okay? I'll call you tomorrow when the boys are up and about."

"Night," Elise calls as she waves goodbye from the far side of her Range Rover's hood. She shakes her head as she drives off. "That bitch is weird," she mutters to herself.

•••

"That's her? You're *sure*?"

"Yeah, Hicks. Elise Abbington," Lawrence responds from the backseat of the Malibu. Hicks glares at him over his shoulder, sniffing for the slightest whiff of bullshit. Ruben's driving his car, which makes him even edgier than usual as they pull out behind the Range Rover. Hicks scribbles down the license plate number in his notepad. At the stop sign, Ruben flicks his left-turn signal on as the Range

Rover makes a right.

"What the hell are you doing? I wanna know where this bitch lives."

"That wasn't the deal," Lawrence chimes in and pushes himself forward from the backseat.

"Look, Larry, I don't trust you, I don't like you, and I sure as hell don't give a rat's ass about whatever deal you and Ruben worked out." Ruben waits at the intersection for a moment, unsure what to do, until Hicks prods him. "Turn right." There's another moment of uncertainty, but Hicks spits out the words, "Drive. The. Fucking. Car," and they turn right. Elise's Range Rover is almost a block ahead of them now but still plainly in view. A few minutes and a couple of turns later, they pass a newly built two-story townhouse where the Range Rover pulls into the garage next to a black Mercedes. Hicks scribbles the address and the Mercedes' plate number in his notebook as Lawrence crumples his body into the smallest, most inconspicuous shape a 6'1" man can muster in the back seat of a '74 Malibu. "There. Now we can call it a night. I got what I came for."

Lawrence is afraid to speak but even more afraid of not warning them, so he whispers from his horribly uncomfortable crouch, "We need to get out of here, *now*. They'll be watching. They're always fucking watching."

"Ain't nobody seen you, get your ass up," Hicks half laughs, half snarls. "You look ridiculous back there. A grown man hiding out like that." Hearing this, Ruben smiles in spite of himself, relieved that Hicks' invective has another target, if only for an evening. "We'll get you back to your people . . . none the wiser."

Twelve miles north, Ruben pulls off Highway 101 into the cracked parking lot of what was once a Foster's Freeze, where dry weeds and errant bits of trash are keeping Lawrence's Honda Civic company. Ruben slides the gearshift into park and turns to the back seat. "I want to thank you, Lawrence. I know you took a risk, but you did a good thing tonight."

Lawrence angrily discards his seatbelt. "You probably just got me killed, you assholes."

"And that's why Ruben here was saying thank—"

Lawrence spits back, "Get fucked, Hicks. And fuck you too, Ruben." He storms off to his car and mutters, "I trusted you fucking pricks," in the direction of nobody in particular, middle finger slung over his shoulder.

Ruben goes to leave the parking lot and Hicks shoots him a withering glance. "What?"

"I only let you drive my car because I don't trust you to keep your buddy Lawrence in line."

Ruben looks back at the older man incredulously, and after a handful of unwavering eye contact, abdicates the driver's seat in exasperation.

•••

Not too much later, Hicks wordlessly pulls into the driveway of the Nor-Cal Motor Paradise and parks the car. Ruben, in between bites of a Double-Double, looks at him quizzically. Hicks tells him, "No, no. You go ahead, finish that burger," so he does. There are only a few bites left anyway.

Ruben dabs thousand-island from the edges of his mouth and asks, "So uh, where exactly are we?"

"Your hotel," Hicks replies as he produces a key card from the inside pocket of his jacket.

"My . . . ?"

"Do you have to be so goddamned dense? Your hotel . . . as in, you're staying here, I'm not. So take your tiger fries and get the fuck out of my car."

"They're animal style—"

"I don't give a fuck what they're called. Take your shit and kick rocks."

"But where are you gonna go?"

Hicks hands Ruben the In-n-Out bag and looks him dead in the eyes. "The less you know, the better." A grin cracks the man's withering gaze for a moment. "Because I'm gonna go do something really fucking stupid."

Ruben stands in the chilly parking lot holding a bag of fries and the key card. Hicks adds sarcastically, "Don't wait up." It isn't until the tail lights of the Malibu fade in the distance that Ruben realizes there's no room number on the key card and the front desk is already closed for the night.

It starts raining.

•••

Elise is floating in jet-black water, staring directly up into a crystal-clear, endless night sky dotted with innumerable stars. The black firmament and the dark water become one another at the horizon, undulating in a continuous loop around her. The glistening stars overhead are reflected just as brilliantly in the water, or perhaps it's the other way around, and she's looking down at the water from the heavens. Whichever way is up no longer matters because she's in the center of it all, floating and weightless, buoyed by the breath in her lungs and the life flowing through her body. The sky and water and she are inextricably connected, the elements flowing not just through her, but from her. Her heart is racing, and her heavy, ragged breath echoes in her ears. She's both exhilarated and at peace, having surrendered all thought and every cell in her body to the waves all around her that rise and fall with her heartbeat. The waves shudder and ripple through her body and she hears a thrumming pulse, resonating from deep within her. It grows louder and more insistent until it hurts, but only for a moment, before something inside her bursts and allows the surging motion to take its course through her body.

The numbing swells rise and fall in time with the waves that shelter her even as they engulf her, and there is no more pain, no more memory or even concept of pain. She's moved beyond sensation into something purer. The surges come faster and faster, her body writhing, then thrashing with them, dancing ecstatically in time with the intertwining of the churning sea and the swirling cosmos. Finally, she is overcome and the sky and the ocean are no longer dark. They're blindingly bright and so is she. Everything is light.

Startled, Elise wakes up from the best climax of her life, alone in bed, blinking in the darkness. She's overcome by how good she feels and starts laughing, more freely than she has in a long time. She feels everything, the dampness of the sweat on her skin, and how much wetter her crotch is beneath her nightie. She feels herself, the warm, slightly sticky nectar between her legs, and relishes it. She brings her hand to her mouth to taste it and then realizes it's jet black. She knows this should alarm her, and for a moment, it does, but she licks it off her fingers anyway. Her tongue is met with a deep, rich taste of flesh and sweat and something else—something wonderful. As good as it tastes, the thought of how the slightest brush of her fingers against her labia felt is even more overwhelming. Her desire to see her OB-GYN about the black fluid between her legs or to wash it out of the sheets floats away in the overwhelming tide of the pleasure she can give herself. She turns and grabs her vibrator, still resting on the bed beside her, coated in her juices. She presses herself against it, grinding blissfully toward another orgasm. Her mind is blank, no fantasies of ex-boyfriends or cute guys from spin class, just an endless darkness of flowing obsidian, coursing through her veins, out from her and into her in an unending cascade of bliss.

She's getting close to coming again when she hears something and snaps out of it. Her reverie was so deep she's not sure what it was, but now she's painfully aware of what she's been doing. Her hand and her vibrator are drenched in viscous black fluid, and reflexively, she feels ashamed, though she's not sure why. She doesn't have time to puzzle it out because there's someone in her house that shouldn't be here. She hears the stranger approach and she runs as quietly as she can into the bathroom and hides behind the shower curtain. There's a window there, but she quickly surmises it's far too small to shimmy out of, and besides, she's on the second floor. It's then she realizes she left her phone on the nightstand.

It's then she realizes she's fucked.

Hicks can hear her, and he knows she's heard him. The abruptly silenced vibrator and the cessation of her moaning is a dead giveaway. Ascending the stairs, he weighs his options and thinks to himself, "Fuck it." He musters his calmest, most reassuring southern drawl and leads with, "Ma'am, I'm sorry to disturb you, but this can't wait."

Silence. He guesses he'd respond the same in her shoes.

"Mrs. Abbington? Elise? I'm not here to rob you or hurt you. I'm here to help you. You may not know it, but there are some dangerous people after you." He pauses on the threshold to her bedroom, at first to let his words sink in and then, once he's flicked the light on, to take in the sight of her bed. The sheets are stained and splattered black where her pelvis would have been resting. It wasn't thick enough to be pure Atramentium, but the translucent black fluid oozes like something alive, almost glistening with even darker flecks in its viscous rivulets. He'd seen a pussy that dripped Atramentium before, but not one possessed by a living, breathing woman. Hicks didn't know exactly what that meant, but he knew it scared the hell out of him.

A cursory once-over of the place makes it clear she's left the bedroom itself, so that leaves only the closet or the bathroom. He grabs her phone from the nightstand, pockets it, and heads for the walk-in closet. "You've probably been experiencing some weird shit lately, right? I know a little about it and I wanna get you the help you need. And I'm sorry, but I had to come in the middle of the night like this because you're being followed. You're being watched by people that want to do you harm. They're after me too." He flicks on the light in the closet and hears her run from the bathroom out to the stairs.

"Ma'am! Hold up there! *Ma'am!*" he shouts into the semi-darkness. She half-stumbles, half-falls down the stairs but picks herself up in time to stay ahead of him. Hicks curses the rod in his leg as he gives chase, because she's already in the garage. By the time he's there, the Range Rover is reversing out, crumpling the Mercedes' driver's-side door, headlights blinding him. He stumbles into the driveway toward his car, blinking like crazy.

The rain falls hard on him, followed abruptly by something much harder. They've found him.

Something that feels like a Louisville Slugger hits him behind the knees and Hicks hits the ground, suddenly feeling every day of his fifty-three years. Someone else kicks him in the head from the right and the second crack of the bat is the last thing he hears or feels before everything goes dark.

•••

Elise keeps looking over her shoulder as she drives, but nobody's following her, at least not that she can tell. It's raining hard and she can barely see the road as she racks her brain for a destination. She's got no wallet, no phone, no nothing, just a white-knuckle grip on the steering wheel and shivers dancing through the whole of her body.

"Someone's after me," she thinks. "Either that guy in the house or the people he was talking about. Or both. Why? Who the fuck am I that people are after me? How is this my life right now?"

She drives on for a minute, shaking and trying to piece her splintered thoughts together. And then it comes to her. Eliott. She yanks the wheel abruptly, sending the car hydroplaning into a mailbox and taking out a little of a hedge as she hops the curb, but she doesn't care. She needs to get to her child. Annika is in the neighborhood, not far at all. She'll have a phone, clean clothes she can borrow, maybe a gun? Elise startles herself with that last thought. She'd always been averse to firearms, but right now, the idea of one is reassuring.

•••

Annika is in her living room, looking at Peter's phone, which she used to photograph his corpse currently decaying in Hefty bags in her garage. She lingers over a picture of Peter's severed head, his disconnected pate resting near his torso, lolling in the blood that's pooled between them. The blood is deep, dark and sticky, not the bright-red stuff from the movies, but something thicker, almost rust colored—real and vital. The eyes of the head rolled back, gazing up at nothing at all, flecked with blood splatter. She's not sure why she felt the need to take these photos, after all, Guillermo had specifically told her to make no record of his presence or the corpse's, but she felt a compulsion to memorialize this moment. It felt important. It is important.

If she stopped to think about it, she'd be amazed at how fast she's inured herself to these kinds of images.

Looking at the man's face, she searches for who he was. There's nothing outwardly remarkable about him, and yet he was betrothed to the Vessel. "What did she see in him?" Annika wonders to herself as she sips her wine and listens to the rain. Part of her wants to go into her garage and remove the body from its wrappings, to see the absence of life and look into those dead eyes and demand an answer.

She notes herself feeling these urges, as if she's watching herself from a distance. The impulses are strange but she wonders, as she catalogs the feelings, why they arouse no revulsion in her, only curiosity. She's gone through the past weeks almost on auto-pilot, watching herself from outside of herself. When the Elder said the Vessel's husband needed to be killed, she accepted it as necessary without reservation. Severing ties to Elise's old life was important he'd said, and not everyone had a marriage as cold and distant as she and Trevor. When the Elder asked his followers to provide a venue for the killing, she volunteered—she *insisted*. All her life, she'd been waiting to be a part of something important, something that mattered, and she was not going to sit on the sidelines if she could help it. And now, all was in motion, and she was a part of it. She'd found what she was looking for at last. She was a part of something amazing.

All at once, her reverie is shattered as headlights shine through the windows surrounding her front door, and she hurriedly puts Peter's phone under the couch cushion, feeling a pang of something like shame as she's suddenly brought back to reality. She opens the door, surprised to see Elise leaning against the doorframe, soaked to the skin, trembling in only a stained nightie streaked with black fluid. "Elise?"

"Please, Annika . . . Can I come in? Where's my son? I need to use your phone. I need—" Elise half-walks, half-falls into the entryway and Annika can barely hold her up.

"Of course, honey. Slow down a minute, though. What happened? Are you all right?"

"There was a man . . . in my house. He told me—" Elise collapses into the couch and can't speak for a moment. The cushions are soft and warm and she wants with all her heart to disappear into them and be safe again. Annika strokes her hair slowly, and somehow this is exactly what she needs.

"I'll get you a towel and some tea. And you can tell me all about it."

Annika leads Elise to another section of the couch, away from her dead husband's phone, and Elise sits there for a while, her head between her knees, shaking off the cold and trying to catch her breath. When she finally dares to open her eyes, Annika is standing over her with a towel, a terry-cloth robe and a piping-hot cup of tea. "Let's get you warmed up, okay? When you're ready, tell me what happened."

She almost flinches as Annika extends the cup to her, but catches herself. The tea is strong and good, smelling of lavender and something else she can't quite place. Annika helps her out of her wet nightie and gets her in the robe. Elise tingles at the feel of the woman's fingertips on her shoulders, but she can't let herself give in to the pleasure of the sensation. Not until she's safe. She catches herself thinking of the woman's smell, wanting to get lost in the touch of her skin, but shakes herself back into focus. "I need, I *really need* to call the police."

"I've already called someone. They're on their way, honey. Everything is going to be all right."

"And El-El-Eliottt?" She hears herself stammering and it makes her want to cry, to look so weak, to be so weak.

"The boys are sleeping. Come on, if we're quiet we can check in on them." Annika walks Elise up the stairway, helping her gingerly as if she was a precious, fragile, porcelain thing and Elise feels herself beginning to catch her breath. Annika cracks the door and the boys are sleeping peacefully, Sam in his bed and Eliott in a sleeping bag on the floor. Elise starts to cry a little, partially in relief because her son is okay and partially in envy, wishing she could just rest, truly rest. Her eyes burn and she feels like she might never fall asleep again. "You see? Everything is going to be okay," Annika whispers and Elise wants to believe her with all her heart. "Come on, you can lie down in my room. Trevor's been in Phoenix for a week now, I could use the company. Does that sound okay?" Elise nods shakily and smiles even more tenuously, because lying in bed with this woman sounds incredible right now.

Annika lays Elise down in the center of her California king mattress and she watches the Vessel, the bearer of all her hopes, roll over into a fetal position, shaking and crying softly. It breaks her heart, but she knows what to do. She and the others will make this right. Annika strokes her hair and whispers softly, "It's all going to be okay, I promise." The Klonopin she dissolved in the tea worked as well on Elise as they did on Peter, and Elise is already drifting into sleep. Annika quietly retreats to the closet and returns with a loaded Beretta M9A1. She clicks the safety off and heads downstairs to wait.

•••

Hicks opens his eyes into darkness. He's someplace small, crumpled uncomfortably in a corner. The space is too small for him to extend his legs, and everything hurts. He wipes some blood from his brow ridge and out of his eye and he can start to make out shapes in the darkness. He's in a closet. The motherfuckers beat him and left him for dead in a closet. It takes him a minute that feels like an hour to prop himself up and find the door handle, his head enveloped by what is probably a winter jacket. He can't hear anything, so he tries the door and opens it gingerly. The hallway, illuminated by the breaking dawn, is blindingly bright in comparison to the darkness of the closet, which makes everything hurt even worse. He's alone in the house as far as he can tell, and he doesn't stick around long enough to find out if he's wrong. He's still got his car keys, and the rain is lightening up with the morning. He's down, but not out.

Hicks figures he'll need Ruben's help to get back in touch with Lawrence as he drives to the Nor-Cal Motor Paradise. Hoping that putting Ruben up in a different motel and joining him there was enough to throw the Heralds off their scent, he pulls into the parking lot of the Nor-Cal Motor Paradise. After an exceptionally painful ascent up the stairs, he produces the extra key from his jacket pocket and lets himself in. The room is dark and Ruben's dead to the world, which is just as well, because Hicks is in no mood to answer the kid's questions. He drops onto the bed and lies there for a moment, staring at the ceiling, too exhausted to make sense of the jumble of thoughts running through his mind. Before he knows it, he's asleep.

•••

Three sharp knocks fall on the door, accompanied with one self-explanatory word: "Housekeeping!" Hicks jolts awake, and instantly remembers how much pain he's in.

"No thanks!" he replies, trying his best not to sound as pissed off as he is about being awoken. The knocks come again.

"Housekeeping!"

"Why hasn't Ruben dragged his sorry ass out of bed yet?" Hicks wonders as he leaves the bed and cracks the door half as far as the chain lock will allow. He glowers at the overweight woman pushing the laundry cart outside their door and spits out, "I said . . . No. Fucking. Thanks." Having grown sufficiently calloused to abuse from guests, she merely shrugs and pushes the cart on toward the next room.

Now that he's fully awake, Hicks can immediately tell something's wrong. "Ruben, kid. Get up." He shakes the covers, but one touch of the shape under the blanket and he knows it's too skinny to be Ruben. He tries to rouse the shape. "Whoever the fuck you are, get your ass up and start explai—" Lawrence's body rolls off the bed away from him, pulling most of the covers off and landing with a thud. The mattress is soaked with blood and Lawrence's dead face looks up at Hicks from the floor on the other side of the bed. His throat's been cut. "Fuck," Hicks mutters under his breath. The Heralds had a busy night last night. He creeps to the bathroom, already fairly certain of what he'll find there.

He's not wrong. Ruben's body is slumped in the tub, still fully clothed. He's been stabbed, many times. His face has been partially smashed in and a dripping gash now occupies the space where his left eye should have been, shreds of bloody flesh dangling at the edges of the wound. The eye now rests in Ruben's ichor-stained lap, just above the edge of the pool of blood that fills the bottom of the tub. Gore has spattered all over the tile of the shower wall, and

Ruben's hands have been cut to ribbons. "Poor kid," Hicks thinks to himself, "but at least he put up a fight." Hicks can't mourn long though because he needs to get as far away from this crime scene as possible, especially since the cleaning lady can place him here and there aren't that many middle-aged men with Southern accents driving '74 Chevy Malibus in Sonoma County.

•••

Elise opens her eyes at last with the vague sensation of emerging from a pleasant dream. She's in the backseat of Annika's Escalade, which is heading for the coast. Eliott is beside her playing video games and Sam is in the front seat pointing at the sea birds circling lazily above them. The midday sun filters through the clouds and lends a warm, gauzy blur to the trees and hillsides that pass by her window. She feels utterly clean. Her skin feels alive and pure, almost virginal. Someone has washed and braided her hair since she last remembers being awake and she's clothed in only a flowing white robe that's loose and soft on her skin, embroidered with symbols that look strangely familiar.

"Where are we?" she asks falteringly.

"Mom, you're awake!" Eliottt exclaims.

"Yeah, sweetie. I'm awake." She laughs at this, although she's not sure why.

Annika smiles in the driver's seat and passes her a cold mug. "Welcome back, Elise, have some juice. Did you rest well?"

"I . . . Yeah, I did. Best sleep I've had in ages actually."

"I'm so glad to hear that. I know you had a tough night."

Elise furrows her brow at this, trying to remember. She was

scared, was someone after her? Whatever the trouble was, it seems impossibly far away now. Trying to recall it feels pointless. After all, who wants to relive a bad dream? The details slip through her fingers every time she tries to grasp them anyway. Whatever fear she feels seems foolish and faraway now in the warm glow of the day.

"But that's over now. We're going to get you some help, so nothing like that ever happens again."

Elise smiles because that sounds so nice, so comforting. "And . . ." She tries to remember her husband's name and surprises herself with how long it takes her to do so. "Peter? Is Peter all right?"

"Yes, Peter is fine. He's away on business, remember?"

Eliottt chimes in as well. "Dad texted me today. He said you should get me a samurai sword for my birthday!"

Annika laughs at this. "Well, right now we need to get your mom taken care of, Eliott. Let's put a pin in the samurai stuff for the moment, okay? Your mom has a big couple of days ahead of her and we need to make sure she has everything she needs. Then we can talk about swords over ice cream, okay?"

"Thank you, Annika. You're . . ." Elise pauses, weighing her words and feeling their import as if for the first time. "You've been a really good friend to me."

"It's nothing, really. My pleasure." The Escalade glides through downtown Bodega Bay serenely, heading out into the hills until it reaches a large modern house with an ocean view. There are several cars in the driveway already and an old man in similar robes to the ones Annika and Elise wear stands at the front door, shepherding several others, all in the same garb, out to greet them. The home is beautiful, the view of the Pacific Ocean is spectacular, and everything is bathed in warm, soft light. The waves crash faintly against the shore in the distance as Annika leads Elise out of the car and into the waiting throng of acolytes and neophytes. They close in around her, and Elise feels something like the guest of honor, which is confusing but wonderful. Everyone is so kind and welcoming. She feels like she could happily lose herself in the warmth of their collective embrace.

"Supptu Kekh," they murmur as they welcome her and lead her inside. Elise has no idea what it means, but when she says it back, they bow their heads and smile or laugh affectionately. Eliott and Sam are led off to another part of the house by the promise of pizza, leaving Elise with the other dozen or so assembled here. The Elder herds everyone toward a large open room probably intended for use as a formal dining room. The room is largely empty, and the absence of a banquet table is compensated for by the presence of a large shape against the far wall, a bulky structure covered by a white sheet. Elise can feel the shape under the sheet, humming and pulsing in time with her breath. The tile floor is gouged and scraped, but otherwise the room is like the rest of the house—immaculate. Once everyone is inside, Annika takes Elise's hand and walks her to the center of the room. Elise feels a little embarrassed by all of these people making a fuss over her.

"What is 'Supptu Kekh?' What does it mean?" she whispers to Annika.

Annika looks into Elise's eyes with rapturous admiration. "Supptu Kekh is mother. Supptu Kekh is you, Elise. You will be mother to us all."

•••

Hicks is glad his room at the Super Value 101 Motor Lodge is on the first floor because, between the ass-kicking he got last night and the rod in his leg, a flight of stairs is about the last thing he needs right now. What he does need, however, he quickly grabs from his room. There's no time to take inventory, but he does allow himself to gulp down a couple of swigs of Wild Turkey and a fistful of ibuprofen. With Ruben and Lawrence dead, his only lead is the house in Bodega Bay. He's seen them use the same place for their ritual a few times, but they usually keep moving once they know he's been sniffing around. He allows himself the foolish hope they still presumed him dead because what did one more bit of foolishness matter now? He has already gotten Ruben killed, so there was precious little left to risk. Of course, there's Hicks' own life in the balance, but that didn't occur to him. His only thought is that if the Heralds believed him dead, they might still be in Bodega Bay. Besides, it's the only lead he had left, so . . .

"Fuck it," Hicks mutters as he slams the door of his Malibu shut and heads toward whatever awaits him in Bodega Bay.

•••

Elise lies on the floor, surrounded by the Heralds of Celestial Ascendancy. They circle her and sing with adoration:

Venth unkhi Supptu Kekh

Khyrr Inkhum Shabba Kekh

Shabba Kekh ek Tharfakh!

She's not sure what it means, but somehow it makes sense. The

Elder turns the pages of the *Astronomicon* gingerly and leads the Heralds in another refrain, but it doesn't matter. The song, the Heralds, all of them soon fade away as the world around Elise goes dark. She's floating again, looking down at an endless obsidian sea, gleaming with the light of countless stars reflected in pitch-black water. She reaches down to touch the water, and it flows toward her outstretched hand. Her hand is as dark as the sea, and the stars are within her fingers, their light a reflection of her own. She trembles as she makes contact with the water, which trembles in response. It roils in time with the beat of her heart and the breath in her body. The fluid rushes through her and she is cleansed by it, all fear, all doubt is swept away in a dark cascade of endless crashing waves.

•••

Hicks drives past the house in Bodega Bay and sees the cars parked outside, so he parks his car about a quarter-mile up the road. He tries to find some tall grass to conceal the car without success. "God fucking damn it," he mutters as he gets out of the car, feeling the stiffness in his left leg. The damp, breezy ocean air and the metal rod in his aching limb don't seem to be getting along particularly well at all. Dispensing with any pretense of subtlety and anticipating the worst, he carries his Sig Sauer P226 MK-25 at his side, fully loaded, safety off.

He approaches the house without incident, which he finds more unnerving than if he'd been met with resistance. He quickly takes the measure of the place, and it doesn't take a rocket-scientist to figure out where they are. The windows of one of the rooms (a dining room, if he had to guess) are glowing brilliantly, even through the blinds. Something is happening, something he hasn't seen before. He approaches the window to try and get a look inside, a burst of light from within shatters the windows, sending shards of glass flying at him along with broken bits of the wooden blinds. By the time Hicks has risen to his knees, he can see that there are no more windows, and part of the wall has also been destroyed.

A woman that was once Elise Abbington, composed completely of Atramentium, floats in the center of the room, encircled by swirling tendrils of the black substance that seems to be both emanating from her and flowing into her. The Heralds are prostrate on the ground now, some are still attempting to chant, but the spiraling streams of viscous blackness are creating a deafening cacophony— the rhythmic sound of countless nails screeching on an infinite number of chalkboards in unison. The sound rips through Hicks' body, pulsing violently and preventing him from gaining his feet, which is just as well, as the tendrils of Atramentium begin lashing out from the woman in wide, slashing arcs.

The Atramentium whiplashes around the room, singing with bursts of unbearable noise, it slices clean through one of the neophytes, cleaving his torso from his right shoulder through his left hip. The two pieces of his body slide off one another slowly, exposing the bloody viscera contained therein. Hicks watches the man's thorax disgorge his entrails onto the floor in a sickening gush of wet splatter, another tendril catches one of the acolytes in the face, sending eyes, sinew, cartilage and bone spraying outward. The acolyte's body stumbling backwards is all that prevents her brain from slithering out of the gaping, blood-drenched hole that used to be her face.

The Heralds panic and start to run, but it does most of them little good. One of them dies screaming, though his death-shriek is muted by the deafening din that fills the room as his leg is shorn off by a flailing wave of black energy. Another is speared through the groin and split like a wishbone, their bowels dropping out of their body through what was once their crotch with an undignified "plop" that sounds almost like a cartoon sound effect. Hicks is rooted to the spot, watching this unfold, momentarily so transfixed he hasn't noticed the cuts all over his face and hands from the shattered shards of the windows. A couple of the more fortunate Heralds exit through the window and run past him in their escape, barely noticing him in their panic-stricken flight. He feels something in his gut though, the hardening of his resolve. If he had time to think it through, he'd recognize the feeling: the confirmation of all of his suspicions about God, that if God exists, he/she/it is a fucking ass-hole.

Hicks gets to his feet amongst the cacophony, his teeth gritted, wincing with pain and effort as climbs through the shattered window. Another Herald runs past him, their robe streaked with freshly spattered gore, and he doesn't even notice. The Elder, his head bowed, still muttering his incantations, is the next to feel an Atramentium tendril, this one stabbing up through his midsection and sending his heart and lungs out of the backside of his shattered rib cage, along with shards of bone and vertebrae and a spray of ichor that stains the wall behind him, leaving a Rorschach blot of human carnage as blood pours out of the old man's torso.

Only one Herald remains alive in the room, a woman on her knees, her robe red with the slaughter of her congregation. The tendrils seem to be more controlled now, circling the floating woman rhythmically. Within the undulating dark liquid that comprises her form are flecks of flickering light. She ripples and pulses, not wholly solid nor liquid, but some unearthly stage of matter between the two.

"Elise? What happened to you?" Hicks screams to be heard over the cacophony around him. He feels like he's in a wind tunnel. "Are you all right?" He nears the woman-shaped thing, he shouts at the top of his lungs, "Mrs. Abbington! Can you hear me? Are you in there?"

The obsidian form looks back at him and replies. "No. Not anymore."

"Then what the fuck are you supposed to be?" Hicks screams over the clamor.

"I am only that which I am," a voice ripples back through his mind.

"Yeah, I figured you'd say some new-age bullshit like that." Hicks snarls back, his words engulfed by the roar of the noise around him. He fires four rounds in rapid succession into whatever this thing is floating in front of him. The bullets pass harmlessly into the floating, flowing form. The noise continues to get louder as he approaches, and the force of the sound feels like a wind buffeting him. Each step toward the being is more difficult than the last. Petulantly raging against his own insignificance, Hicks keeps firing until the clip is empty, his hands aching from the recoil and the screaming noise that shakes his bones. The floating shape regards him as he approaches, fighting through the awful cacophony that makes every step an excruciating effort. For every inch he gains toward the thing, he's pushed back almost as far, but he's close now ... almost close enough to touch it. He reaches toward it, trembling fingers only a few inches away. The noise pulses out in a concentrated burst, sending him flying backwards into the demolished section of the wall.

And then everything is silent.

•••

The noise has stopped, and Annika raises her head at last. Elise is floating majestically in the center of the room, a thing composed of Atrentium, but also a thing commanding it. The ebon, humanoid form containing both absolute darkness and pinpoints of blinding luminescence is the most beautiful thing she's ever seen. She wipes off the blood splattering her face and beholds the entire scene—the Master floating in the center of the room, resplendent and radiant, surrounded by the mutilated corpses of the Heralds, their brains, entrails and limbs strewn haphazardly around the room.

"You—you saved me," Annika stammers.

"Just as you saved me," the Master responds, the words, the concepts of the words echoing and vibrating peacefully through Annika's mind and body.

Not knowing how to respond, Annika cautiously rises to her feet. "What now, Master?" The Master turns her black head toward Annika, and instantly she knows what she must do. She strips off her robe, and now naked, hurries toward the other room where Eliott and Sam are hiding under the bed, huddled together as they tremble in fear. "Boys? You can come out now. It's all over. Everything is going to be okay."

The two boys, crying, emerge from their hiding place and run into Annika's arms. "Shhh now. It's going to be okay, guys. I just need you to be brave for me. You can do that, right?" Annika leads them back through the house to the Master, tousling their hair.

Entering the dining room, the boys are too shocked at the sight of the carnage and the Master to speak. At the far side of the abattoir, the cradle is now revealed, its battered and bent shell wide open, emitting a swirling cascade of black light that casts an unearthly glow on the horrific scene of slaughter around it.

"Mom?" Eliott finally manages.

"Yes and no," The Master replies silently.

"Is this— I thought, I thought you would give birth to the Master?" Annika tries to form the question she's been mulling over.

The echo in her mind replies, "I did give birth. But to myself. There is little the Elder understood."

Annika tries to puzzle this through, but her other question seems more pressing. "So . . . what now? Are you taking us with you? To where you came from? That was the prophecy, wasn't it? The promise?"

The black light from the cradle grows more powerful, its field widening. The Master opens her arms and the light from her grows brighter, a dark luminosity that defies reason and description. The light beaming out from her engulfs most of the room.

•••

Hicks, half-conscious, watches this from the rubble of the outer dining room wall in disbelief. It takes every bit of effort to stay conscious and observe as the light of the darkness engulfs the room in a cold, harsh glare. A nude woman leads two boys into its source, the former Mrs. Elise Abbington. The swirling energies from the cradle wash out over them all, growing brighter and brighter until everything is subsumed by it.

By the time Hicks' vision returns, he's alone, surrounded by the corpses of the Heralds in various states of dismemberment and all is silent except for the distant noise of the waves crashing against the shore and Hicks finally allows himself to close his eyes.

EPILOGUE

"35034-061- HICKS, EDGAR?"

Hicks' ears prick up and he stands wearily, leaning on the bars of his cell. Four days and a lot of stitches later and he's in more pain than when he was getting his ass kicked, either time. The paper-thin jail mattress hadn't helped his back much either. "Yessir."

"You made bail, Hicks. You're free to go."

Hicks has been in this situation more than enough times to know better than to show any kind of reaction one way or another, especially because the cop who comes to fetch him is young and eager. The young and eager ones, they're the worst, the most brutal, because they have something to prove. So Hicks simply nods and walks out, his gait stiff and slow. The rod in his left leg is especially cold today, which never means anything good.

Hicks walks past the holding cells filled with the usual assortment of drunks, hookers, gangbangers and wife-beaters you find in County, with no idea of what awaits him. With Ruben dead, he doesn't know anyone in Northern California, at least nobody that would give enough of a rat's ass about him to post his bail.

He emerges into the lobby area with his plastic bag of possessions. and is immediately approached by an obviously wealthy couple who look to be in their sixties. The woman approaches him, trying to maintain her decorum, but there's a vein of hysteria beneath it. "Mr. Hicks? I'm Dorthea Littlebaum. I hope you don't think it too forward, posting your bail, but my husband Alan and I are in need of someone with your skillset. You came very highly recommended."

Hicks nods his head. "Mr. and Mrs. Littlebaum, pleased to meetcha."

Alan, a large man with a strangely high voice extends his hand. "You see, Mr. Hicks, it's about our daughter, Paige. We have reason to believe she's in some sort of trouble."

Hicks half-smiles. "If you paid my bail, it must be bad. Why don't you tell me all about it . . . *after* you get my car out of impound.

A.S. Coomer is a writer and musician. Books include *Memorabilia*, *The Fetishists*, *Shining the Light*, *The Devil's Gospel*, *The Flock Unseen*, and others.

www.ascoomer.com

Lucas Mangum is the author of several books including *Gods of the Dark Web*, *Mania*, and the Splatterpunk Award-nominated *Saint Sadist*. His work has appeared in several anthologies, most notably *The Big Book of Blasphemy* from Necro Publications and *V-Wars: Shockwaves* from IDW Publishing. World Horror Grandmaster Brian Keene praised Mangum's debut, *Flesh and Fire*, calling it "*Supernatural* with balls." You can get a PDF of that book for free by clicking on the store link at lucasmangum.com. You can also find him on Twitter @RealLucasMangum where he tweets dubious writing advice and opinions on both classic and contemporary horror movies. He lives in Texas with his family.

Matt Harvey is a Bay Area native who currently resides in San Luis Obispo, California with his wife Camilla and their extremely fluffy dog Astra. When not writing or cataloging his comic book and vinyl collections, he spends most of his time playing in underground metal bands like Exhumed, Gruesome, and Pounder.

www.mattharveymustbedestroyed.com
Facebook.com/mattharveymustbedestroyed
Instagram @mattharveymustbedestroyed

Other Grindhouse Press Titles

#666__*Satanic Summer* by Andersen Prunty

#069__*Depraved 4* by Bryan Smith

#068__*Worst Laid Plans: An Anthology of Vacation Horror* edited by
Samantha Kolesnik

#067__*Deathtripping: Collected Horror Stories* by Andersen Prunty

#066__*Depraved* by Bryan Smith

#065__*Crazytimes* by Scott Cole

#064__*Blood Relations* by Kristopher Triana

#063__*The Perfectly Fine House* by Stephen Kozeniewski and
Wile E. Young

#062__*Savage Mountain* by John Quick

#061__*Cocksucker* by Lucas Milliron

#060__*Luciferin* by J. Peter W.

#059__*The Fucking Zombie Apocalypse* by Bryan Smith

#058__*True Crime* by Samantha Kolesnik

#057__*The Cycle* by John Wayne Comunale

#056__*A Voice So Soft* by Patrick Lacey

#055__*Merciless* by Bryan Smith

#054__*The Long Shadows of October* by Kristopher Triana

#053__*House of Blood* by Bryan Smith

#052__*The Freakshow* by Bryan Smith

#051__*Dirty Rotten Hippies and Other Stories* by Bryan Smith

#050__*Rites of Extinction* by Matt Serafini

#049__*Saint Sadist* by Lucas Mangum

#048__*Neon Dies at Dawn* by Andersen Prunty

CPSIA information can be obtained
at www.ICGtesting.com
Printed in the USA
BVHW030559231220
596061BV00004B/4